Out of This World

Authors

Mary Lind
Pam Knecht
Bill Dodge

Ana Williams
Arthur Wiebe

Editors

Arthur Wiebe
Betty Cordel

Judith Hillen

Illustrations

Sheryl Mercier

Brenda Dahl

Consultant

Dr. Larry A. Lebofsky
Senior Research Scientist
Lunar and Planetary Laboratory
University of Arizona

i

AIMS is committed to remaining at the cutting edge of providing integrated math/science studies that are user friendly, educationally sound, developmentally appropriate, and aligned with the recommendations from national education documents.

Out Of This World has been revised in order to maintain this high standard. In this revision you will notice that many of our activities have been updated due to the tremendous amount of newly acquired information from space research. We are proud to have had Dr. Larry Lebofsky review the entire manuscript to check its accuracy and applicability. To illustrate our efforts of aligning our activities with national documents, we have included a listing of the *Benchmarks for Science Literacy* (American Association for the Advancement of Science) and the *Curriculum and Evaluation Standards for School Mathematics* (National Council of Teachers of Mathematics) which apply to the activities in this publication. To allow students and teachers the opportunity for personal research, many new titles have been included in the Additional Resources section of the book.

This book contains materials developed by the AIMS Education Foundation. **AIMS** (**A**ctivities **I**ntegrating **M**athematics and **S**cience) began in 1981 with a grant from the National Science Foundation. The non-profit AIMS Education Foundation publishes hands-on instructional materials (books and the monthly *AIMS* Magazine) that integrate curricular disciplines such as mathematics, science, language arts, and social studies. The Foundation sponsors a national program of professional development through which educators may gain both an understanding of the AIMS philosophy and expertise in teaching by integrated, hands-on methods.

ISBN **1-881431-43-6**

Printed in the United States of America

Project 2061 Benchmarks

The following is a listing of the *Benchmarks* as taken from *Benchmarks for Science Literacy* (American Association for the Advancement of Science) which apply in total or in part to the activities in *Out Of This World*.

- *Scientific knowledge is subject to modification as new information challenges prevailing theories and as a new theory leads to looking at old observations in a new way.*

- *Science is an adventure that people everywhere can take part in, as they have for many centuries.*

- *Clear communication is an essential part of doing science. It enables scientists to inform others about their work, expose their ideas to criticism by other scientists, and stay informed about scientific discoveries around the world.*

- *Numbers and shapes–and operations on them– help to describe and predict things about the world around us.*

- *Important contributions to the advancement of science, mathematics, and technology have been made by different kinds of people, in different cultures, at different times.*

- *No matter who does science and mathematics or invents things, or when or where they do it, the knowledge and technology that result can eventually become available to everyone in the world.*

- *Scientists are employed by colleges and universities, business and industry, hospitals, and many government agencies. Their places of work include offices, classrooms, laboratories, farms, factories, and natural field settings ranging from space to the ocean floor.*

- *Mathematics is helpful in almost every kind of human endeavor–from laying bricks to prescribing medicine or drawing a face. In particular, mathematics has contributed to progress in science and technology for thousands of years and still continues to do so.*

- *Technology is essential to science for such purposes as access to outer space and other remote locations, sample collection and treatment, measurement, data collection and storage, computation, and communication of information.*

- *Technology enables scientists and others to observe things that are too small or too far away to be seen without them and to study the motion of objects that are moving very rapidly or are hardly moving at all.*

- *Telescopes magnify the appearance of some distant objects in the sky, including the moon and the planets. The number of stars that can be seen through telescopes is dramatically greater than can be seen by the unaided eye.*

- *Stars are like the sun, some being smaller and some larger, but so far away that they look like points of light.*

- *The sun is a medium-sized star located near the edge of a disk-shaped galaxy of stars, part of which can be seen as a glowing band of light that spans the sky on a very clear night. The universe contains many billions of galaxies, and each galaxy contains many billions of stars. To the naked eye, even the closest of these galaxies is not more than a dim, fuzzy spot.*

- *The sun is many thousands of times closer to the earth than any other star. Light from the sun takes a few minutes to reach the earth, but light from the next nearest star takes a few years to arrive. The trip to that star would take the fastest rocket thousands of years. Some distant galaxies are so far away that their light takes several billion years to reach the earth. People on earth, therefore, see them as they were that long ago in the past.*

- *Nine planets of very different sizes, composition, and surface features move around the sun in nearly circular orbits. Some planets have a great variety of moons and even flat rings of rock and ice particles orbiting around them. Some of these planets and moons show evidence of geological activity. The earth is orbited by one moon, many artificial satellites, and debris.*

- *We live on a relatively small planet, the third from the sun in the only system of planets definitely known to exist (although other, similar systems may be discovered in the universe).*

- *Everything on or anywhere near the earth is pulled toward the earth's center by gravitational force.*

- The earth is one of several planets that orbit the sun, and the moon orbits around the earth.

- The sun's gravitational pull holds the earth and other planets in their orbits, just as the planets' gravitational pull keeps their moons in orbit around the sun.

- Every object exerts gravitational force on every other object. The force depends on how much mass the objects have and on how far apart they are.

- Computations (as on calculators) can give more digits than make sense or are useful.

- Tables and graphs can show how values of one quantity are related to values of another.

- The graphic display of numbers may help to show patterns such as trends, varying rates of change, gaps, or clusters. Such patterns sometimes can be used to make predictions about the phenomena being graphed.

- It takes two numbers to locate a point on a map or any other flat surface. The numbers may be two perpendicular distances from a point, or an angle and a distance from a point.

- Telescopes reveal that there are many more stars in the night sky than are evidenct to the unaided eye, the surface of the moon has many craters and mountains, the sun has dark spots, and Jupiter and some other planets have their own moons.

- Models are often used to think about processes that happen too slowly, too quickly, or on too small a scale to observe directly, or that are too vast to be changed deliberately, or that are potentially dangerous.

- Different models can be used to represent the same thing. What kind of a model to use and how complex it should be depends on its purpose. The usefulness of a model may be limited if it is too simple or if it is needlessly complicated. Choosing a useful model is one of the instances in which intuition and creativity come into play in science, mathematics, and engineering.

- Geometric figures, number sequences, graphs, diagrams, sketches, number lines, maps, and stories can be used to represent objects, events, and processes in the real world, although such representations can never be exact in every detail.

- In something that consists of many parts, the parts usually influence one another.

Students should:
- Use, interpret, and compare numbers in several equivalent forms such as integers, fractions, decimals, and percents.

- Calculate the circumferences and areas of rectangles, triangles, and circles, and the volumes of rectangular solids.

- Find the mean and median of a set of data.

- Estimate distances and travel times from maps and the actual size of objects from scale drawings.

- Decide what degree of precision is adequate and round off the result of calculator operations to enough significant figures to reasonably reflect those of the inputs.

- Organize information in simple tables and graphs and identify relationships they reveal.

- Read simple tables and graphs produced by others and describe in words what they show.

- Use numerical data in describing and comparing objects and events.

- Understand writing that incorporates circle charts, bar and line graphs, two-way data tables, diagrams, and symbols.

- Find and describe locations on maps with rectangular and polar coordinates.

NCTM Standards

Below is a listing of the standards found in the National Council of Teachers of Mathematics (NCTM) publication *Curriculum and Evaluation Standards for School Mathematics* which are addressed in total or in part in this publication.

The mathematics curriculum should include numerous and varied experiences with problem solving as a method of inquiry and application so that students can–

- *develop and apply a variety of strategies to solve problems, with emphasis on multistep and nonroutine problems;*

- *generalize solutions and strategies to new problem situations;*

- *acquire confidence in using mathematics meaningfully.*

The study of mathematics should include opportunities to communicate so that students can–

- *model situations using oral, written, concrete, pictorial, graphical, and algebraic methods;*

- *use the skills of reading, listening, and viewing to interpret and evaluate mathematical ideas.*

The mathematics curriculum should include the investigation of mathematical connections so that students can–

- *see mathematics as an integrated whole:*

- *apply mathematical thinking and modeling to solve problems that arise in other disciplines, such as art, music, psychology, science, and business.*

The mathematics curriculum should include the continued development of number and number relationships so that students can–

- *understand, represent, and use numbers in a variety of equivalent forms (integer, fraction, decimal, percent, exponential, and scientific notation) in real-world and mathematical problem situations;*

- *develop number sense for whole numbers, fractions, decimals, integers, and rational numbers.*

The mathematics curriculum should develop the concepts underlying computation and estimation in various contexts so that students can–

- *select and use an appropriate method for computing from among mental arithmetic, paper-and-pencil, calculator, and computer;*

- *use computation, estimation, and proportions to solve problems;*

- *use estimation to check the reasonableness of results.*

The mathematics curriculum should include the study of geometry of one, two, and three dimensions in a variety of situations so that students can–

- *identify, describe, compare, and classify geometric figures.*

The mathematics curriculum should include extensive concrete experiences using measurement so that students can–

- *extend their understanding of the process of measurement;*

- *select appropriate units and tools to measure to the degree of accuracy required in a particular situation.*

Math/ Science Processes

Activity	Applying Formulas	Attributes	Averaging	Calculators	Decimals	Estimating and Predicting	Geometry	Graphing	Measurement: length	Measurement: time	Measurement: angles	Percent	Problem Solving	Reading / Interpreting Tables	Rounding	Set Theory	Whole Number Operations
Can You Planet		X						X						X		X	X
Planetary Facts								X					X	X		X	
Spacing Out the System					X	X			X				X	X	X		X
Size It Up				X		X	X		X				X	X	X		X
Planetary Scavenger Hunt				X	X	X			X				X		X		
Extraterrestrial Excursions				X	X	X							X		X		X
How Long Does It Take To Say Hello?	X			X		X							X		X		X
Space Talk Message				X		X							X		X		X
Weight In Space				X	X	X			X						X		X
Galactic Games			X	X					X	X			X	X	X		X
Planet Trivia													X				
Phone Home							X					X					
Space Capsule								X					X				
Around The Planets In How Many Days?	X		X						X					X	X		X
Round And Round							X		X								
The Moon Shines Bright			X						X		X			X			
Stars In The Milky Way Galaxy			X	X		X			X	X			X				X
It All Depends On Your Point Of View						X	X	X	X								

Table of Contents

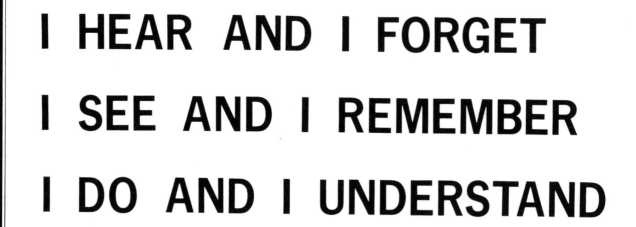

I HEAR AND I FORGET

I SEE AND I REMEMBER

I DO AND I UNDERSTAND

–Chinese Proverb

The Earth and Her Neighbors

The word planet comes from the Greek word planetai, meaning wanderers. To the ancient peoples, the planets in their orbits seemed to move around the sky. The Greeks and Romans named the planets after mythological gods and goddesses. The symbols used to represent the planets often reflect these names.

Mercury: Mercury, closest to the sun is a small, dense, fast-moving planet. It circles the sun in a mere 88 Earth days. The winged helmet and snake-entwined staff of Mercury, the messenger of the Roman gods, can be seen in the symbol for this planet.

Venus: The thick acid clouds which surround Venus reflect sunlight and we see it as the lovely morning and evening "star." Venus was named for the Roman goddess of love and beauty and its symbol, a hand mirror, is also the universal symbol for women.

Earth: The planet we know best orbits within the "ecosphere," just the right distance from the sun to provide us with the temperatures and water necessary for our forms of life. The tilt of its axis gives us our seasons. The symbol for Earth is the Greek sign for sphere. Earth is the only planet not named for an ancient god.

Mars: The reddish mineral covering Mars gives it its name, the Red Planet. Because of its color, it was named for the Roman god of war who was covered with blood. His shield and spear form the planet's symbol which is also the universal sign for man. Mars also tilts on its axis, giving it seasons. Since Mars takes twice as long to circle the sun, its seasons are twice as long as Earth's.

Jupiter:

Jupiter, the largest planet, is aptly named for the king of the Roman gods and symbolized by his lightning bolt. Jupiter fascinates us with its 16 known moons, swirling poisonous gases, and Great Red Spot. In this spot, more than three times the size of the Earth, a giant storm has raged for hundreds of years. Voyagers 1 and 2 detected three faint rings.

Saturn:

Early astronomers described Saturn's rings as "ears." This beautiful planet is a huge, floating ball of gas. Voyager's flyby shows at least 18 moons. Titan, the largest, is bigger than Mercury and has its own atmosphere. Because of its slow movement, Saturn was named for the Roman god of reaping or time whose symbol is a sickle.

Uranus:

Ancient man could not see this seventh planet or any beyond because they did not have telescopes or binoculars. Following its discovery in 1781, astronomers named Uranus for the Roman god who was father to Saturn and grandfather to Jupiter. Its symbol is the sign for the metal platinum. As Uranus orbits the sun, it spins rapidly on its side, its axis always pointing in the same direction. In 1986, Voyager 2 discovered 10 of Uranus' 15 known moons and several more rings.

Neptune:

A strange pull on the planet Uranus gave astronomers the idea that Neptune existed. Discovered in 1846, the new planet was named for the Roman god of the sea. Its symbol is his fishing spear, the trident. Little is known about the smallest of the gas giants. It has eight moons and faint rings.

Pluto:

Pluto was named for the god of the underworld. It was discovered in 1930, the only planet found in the twentieth century. The Pl of Pluto is its symbol, and is also the initials of Percival Lowell, the first man to predict its existence. Because of its distance from the sun, Pluto's orbit is the most elliptical or oval-shaped of the planets and at times is actually closer than Neptune. Pluto's moon, Charon, is nearly as large as Pluto and some scientists consider it a double planet.

Can You Planet?

Topic Area
Planets

Introductory Statement
Students will learn about various aspects of the planets and their relationships with one another by using tables of planetary facts, Venn diagrams, and drawings of the planets themselves.

Math
Using attributes
Using whole number operations
Using Venn diagrams and set theory
Using inequalities: larger, smaller
Using tables

Science
Astronomy
    planets

Math/Science Processes
Classifying
Comparing data
Predicting and inferring
Applying and generalizing
Drawing conclusions

Materials
Student activity sheets
Scissors
Pencils
Crayons or markers

Key Question
How can we classify the nine planets?

Background Information
    Much has been discovered about our planets as a result of information gathered by Voyagers 1 and 2. Students should be encouraged to look for newspaper and magazine articles which continue to report on new information about our solar system. For example, it was only in September 1991 that some of the newly discovered moons were named.

Management
1. Divide the class into pairs or cooperative learning groups for this activity. Alternate between small group activity and whole group discussions. The last part of the activity may be done in small groups with copies of the planets or as a whole class activity with one copy of the planets.
2. If desired, planet names can be attached to the Venn diagram with paste or tacky adhesive. The tacky adhesive is useful because the titles can be moved if inaccurately placed.

Procedure
1. Discuss with students what they already know about the planets. (total number [nine], appearance, distance from the earth, etc.) Have them tell their sources of information whenever possible.
2. Discuss the *Key Question:* Using Venn diagrams, how can we classify the nine planets? [size, appearance, having moons, etc.]
3. Choose any two table headings for the circles of the Venn diagram. Fill in the appropriate planet names.
4. Use the information from *Planetary Facts.* Color in the proper spaces for the first three attributes. Guide the students to choose three more attributes with which to classify the planets. Have groups compare their results and discuss any differences.
5. Using the two-circle and three-circle Venn diagrams, write the names of the planets in the appropriate places. As a whole class, discuss similarities and differences of the planets from information recorded on the Venn diagrams.
6. Using the *Planetary Facts* and the cutout sun and planets, have students place the planets in the proper order from the sun. Emphasize that order, not distance, is important in this activity.
7. With the whole class, make a list of what has been learned.

Discussion
Using the Venn diagrams:
1. Which planets are larger than the earth?
2. Which planets have moons?
3. Which planets have days longer than 24 hours?
4. Which planet fits all three categories?
5. Which planets have no moons?
6. Which planets are smaller than the earth?
7. What percent of the planets have moons?
8. What percent of the planets are smaller than the earth?
9. Which planets have both moons and rings?

Using the Planetary Facts chart:
1. Which planet has the most moons?
2. What is the total number of moons?
3. What is the average number of moons?
4. Which two planets are the closet in size?

Extensions
1. Enlarge the Venn diagrams so that they will accommodate the cutouts of the planets. Arrange the planets by a variety of attributes such as
   • smallest to largest
   • longest day to shortest day
   • no moons to most moons
   Be sure students label each continuum clearly: which is smallest, etc.

3

Curriculum Correlations

Language Arts:
   Have students do research reports on individual planets. The *National Geographic* is an excellent source.

Art:
   Let each group choose a planet to make in papier-mâché by covering a balloon. Have students research the visual characteristics of their planet to represent it as accurately as possible without regard to its size in relation to other planets. Challenge students to create unique ways to show features such as the rings!

CAN YOU PLANET?

Name: _____

PLANETARY FACTS

	Approximate Diameter	Approximate Period of Rotation	Moons	Rings ?
Mercury	4,900 km	59 days [176 days]*	0	No
Venus	12,100 km	243 days [117 days]*	0	No
Earth	12,800 km	23 hours, 56 minutes	1	No
Mars	6,800 km	24 hours, 37 minutes	2	No
Jupiter	143,000 km	9 hours, 55 minutes	16	Yes
Saturn	120,600 km	10 hours, 39 minutes	18	Yes
Uranus	51,100 km	17 hours, 14 minutes	15	Yes
Neptune	49,500 km	16 hours, 7 minutes	8	Yes
Pluto	2,300 km	6 days, 9 hours	1	No

* length of day sunrise to sunrise

CAN YOU PLANET?

⭐ Sort out the planets. Next to each planet's name, color in those spaces that are true. Use this information to place the planets on the Venn Diagram.

Planetary Facts Helping Table

	Larger than Earth	Has Ring(s)	Has Moon(s)
Mercury			
Venus			
Earth			
Mars			
Jupiter			
Saturn			
Uranus			
Neptune			
Pluto			

More Planetary Facts (Venn Again)

Mercury			
Venus			
Earth			
Mars			
Jupiter			
Saturn			
Uranus			
Neptune			
Pluto			

CAN YOU PLANET?

Name: _____

Use the information from the chart to place the planets in the correct circle or intersection of circles.

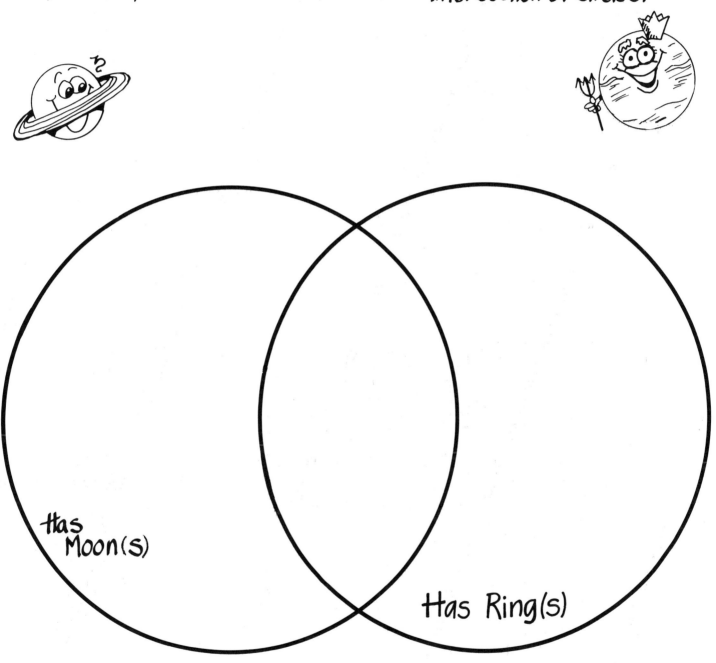

Has Moon(s)

Has Ring(s)

CAN YOU PLANET?

Use the information from the chart to place the planets in the correct circle or intersection of circles.

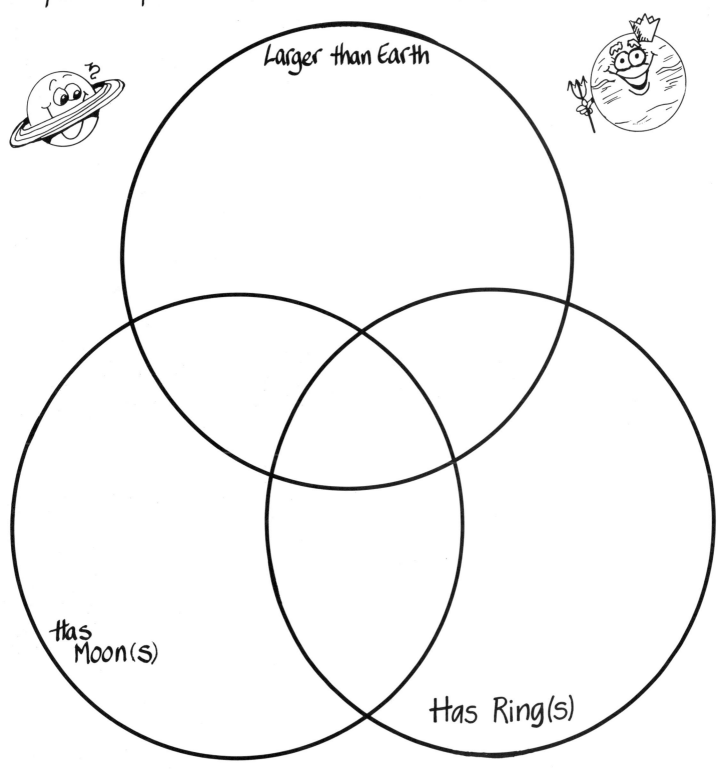

Larger than Earth

Has Moon(s)

Has Ring(s)

CAN YOU PLANET?

Name:_____

Use the Venn Diagram or chart to answer the following questions.

1. Which planets are larger than Earth?_____
_____

2. Which two planets are closest in size?_____ _____

3. What percent of the planets are smaller than Earth?_____

4. Which planets have moons?_____
_____

5. Which planet has the most moons?_____

6. What is the total number of known moons in our solar system?_____

7. What is the average number of moons per planet?_____

8. Which planets fit into all three categories?_____

9. Which planets have days which are longer than 24 hours?
_____

Think of two more questions you can ask your classmates. Write them below.

NAME: _____

HOW MANY MOONS?

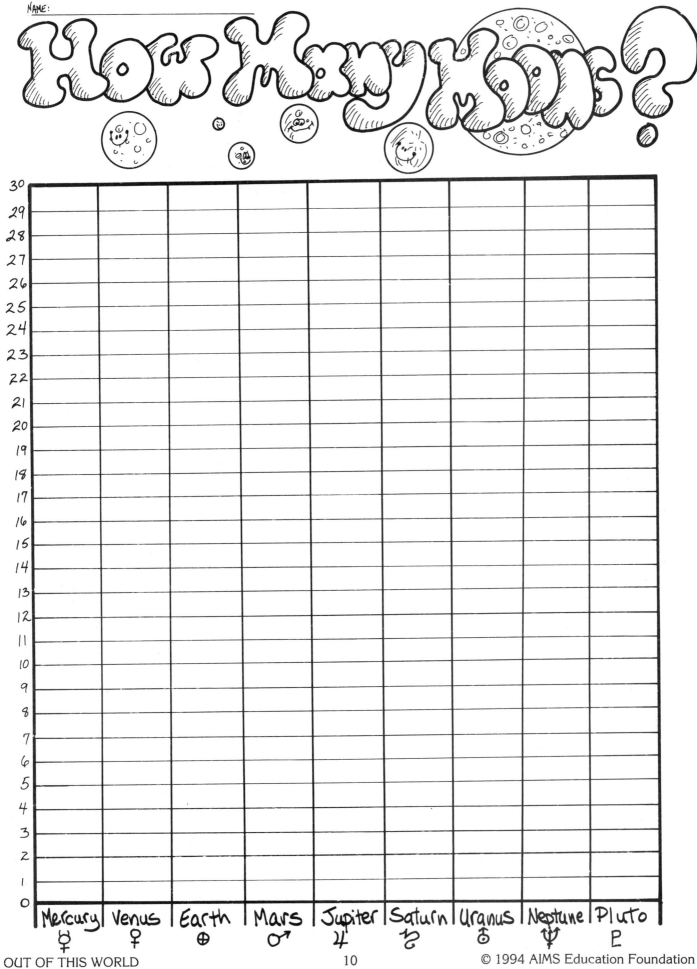

	Mercury ☿	Venus ♀	Earth ⊕	Mars ♂	Jupiter ♃	Saturn ♄	Uranus ♅	Neptune ♆	Pluto ♇
30									
29									
28									
27									
26									
25									
24									
23									
22									
21									
20									
19									
18									
17									
16									
15									
14									
13									
12									
11									
10									
9									
8									
7									
6									
5									
4									
3									
2									
1									
0									

What's My SIZE?

GRAPH THE DIAMETERS OF THE PLANETS.

Kilometers	0	10,000	20,000	30,000	40,000	50,000	60,000	70,000	80,000	90,000	100,000	110,000	120,000	130,000	140,000	150,000	160,000
Mercury																	
Venus																	
Earth																	
Mars																	
Jupiter																	
Saturn																	
Uranus																	
Neptune																	
Pluto																	

11

THE SOLAR SYSTEM

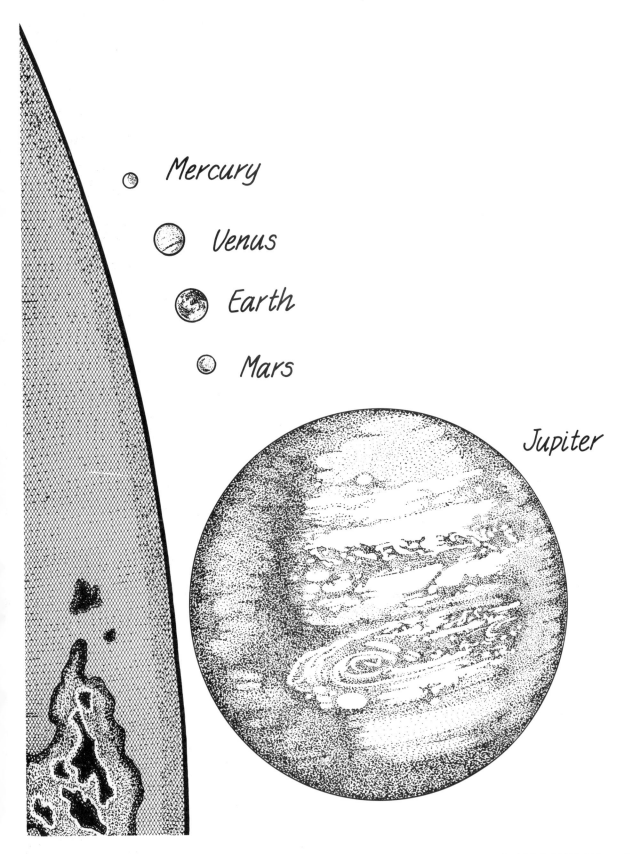

Mercury

Venus

Earth

Mars

Jupiter

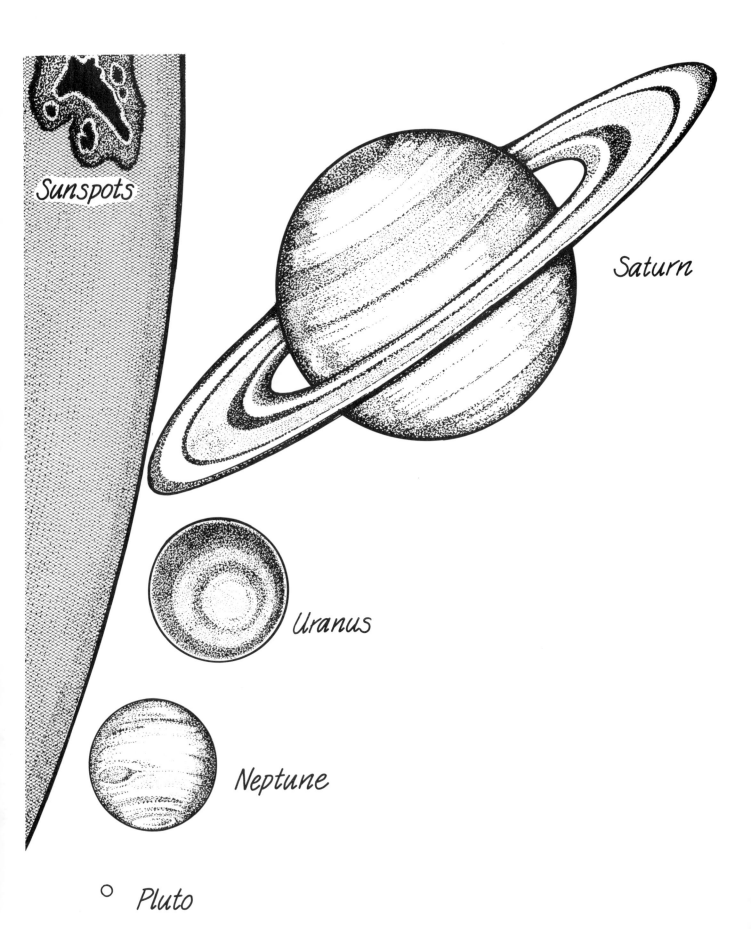

Sunspots

Saturn

Uranus

Neptune

° Pluto

PLANETARY FACTS

(Venn Again)

Topic Area
Planets

Introductory Statement
Students will choose three areas of knowledge about the nine planets and generate a Venn diagram from that information. Students will create graphs to show what they have learned.

Math
Graphing
Using Venn diagrams
Using computation
Problem solving

Science
Astronomy
    planets

Science Processes
Classifying
Comparing data
Interpreting data
Predicting and inferring
Applying and generalizing
Drawing conclusions

Materials
Research materials or tables of information
Graph paper

Key Question
What are some other types of information about the planets we can use to make Venn diagrams?

Background Information
    Students should use the information from *Can You Planet?*, information included in this activity, and any other available planetary resource information to generate categories for the Venn diagram. Students could research various topics and create a table like the one used in *Can You Planet?*, or the teacher could provide additional tables of information.

Management
1. Time for this activity will vary depending on whether students are using the tables which are provided or need to do research to gather data.
2. Students can easily work in small groups to gather data, generate the Venn diagram, and create tables and graphs.
3. *Planetary Facts* from *Can You Planet?* may be used as a preliminary step to creating the Venn diagram.

Procedure
1. Students will choose three topic areas to formulate a Venn diagram.
2. Students will group the nine planets according to the topics chosen.
3. Students will generate discussion questions for classmates regarding their Venn diagram.
4. Students will create a large class Venn diagram to describe their information.
5. Students will graph the information.
6. Students will formulate the mathematical questions using information from the three topic areas they have chosen.

Discussion
1. Which areas did you choose to display in the Venn diagram?
2. Were there some areas that were easier to use in a Venn diagram than others? Explain.
3. What kind of questions can you ask about each of the topic areas?
4. Were you able to create graphs for all topic areas?
5. What value do you find in putting your information into a Venn diagram? Explain.

Extensions
    Make Venn diagrams covering other topic areas in addition to the planets.

PLANETARY FACTS

TERMS

Information about our solar system is constantly changing. New information is being obtained through photographs and other data sent back by Voyager 2. Space telescopes should increase our knowledge even more.

Diameter:

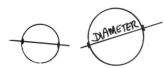

This is the length of a line passed through the middle of a sphere. The larger the diameter, the larger the planet or sphere.

Moons:

This is the number of natural satellites a planet has. Some planets have no moons and some probably have moons we have yet to discover.

Length of Day:

Except for Mercury and Venus, this is very close to how long it takes the planet to rotate once on its axis. Time for all the planets is based on Earth's time.

Length of Year:

This is the amount of time it takes a planet to make one complete orbit around the sun.

Distance from the sun and Earth:

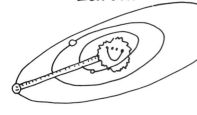

These are measured in millions of kilometers. The distances given are the average distances a planet is orbiting from the sun or the earth. As the orbits of the planet are elliptical rather than circular, a planet will sometimes be closer and sometimes farther in the course of the year.

Mass:

This is the amount of material that something contains. Mass and weight are not the same things. An object acquires weight due to the pull of gravity. A person or object is weightless in space but still has mass. For comparison, the mass of the earth is considered as 1 and other planets' masses are in relation to that.

PLANETARY FACTS

TERMS

Density:

Density tells how tightly mass is packed and is determined by the mass of an object divided by its volume. A basket of feathers has the same volume as a basket of lead but the lead is denser, and so would have a greater mass. The inner planets have a density greater than that of water and would sink in a giant ocean of water. The outer planets are more gaseous and so less dense. Saturn has a density less than water and would float.

Surface Gravity:

Gravity is the force that pulls or holds an object to a planet. The more mass a planet has, the greater its pull and the more you would weigh there. Yet, you would weigh just over two and one half times greater on Jupiter, not 3/8 times because gravitational pull lessens with distance. Jupiter's gaseous surface is far from its massive center.

PLANETARY FACTS

	Distance from Earth in Millions of Km	Distance from Sun in Millions of Km	Density	Mass	Temperature	Gravity	Length of Year
Mercury	91.7	57.9	5.5	0.055	-170° to 350°c	0.39	88 days
Venus	41.4	108.2	5.2	0.815	465°C surface	0.91	225 days
Earth	0	149.6	5.5	1.0	15°C avg. surface	1	365 days
Mars	78.3	227.9	3.9	0.11	-23°C avg. surface	0.38	687 days
Jupiter	628.7	778.3	1.3	318	-150°C at cloud tops	2.60	11.9 years
Saturn	1277	1,427	0.7	95.2	-180°C at cloud tops	1.07	29.5 years
Uranus	2721	2,870	1.3	15	-210°C at cloud tops	0.90	84 years
Neptune	4347	4,497	1.6	17	-220°C at cloud tops	1.15	165 years
Pluto	5,750	5,900	2.1	0.002	-220°C avg. surface	0.03	248 years

PLANETARY FACTS

19

Spacing Out the System

Topic Area
Planets

Introductory Statement
Students will determine the relative distance of the planets in order to construct a model solar system.

Math
Using computation
Rounding
Estimating
Problem solving
Measuring
    length

Science
Astronomy
    planets

Math/Science Processes
Observing
Recording data
Interpreting data
Inferring
Making and testing hypotheses
Applying and generalizing

Materials
Pencils
Calculators
Metric rulers and tapes
Trundle wheel
12" x 18" paper
Optional: seeds and nuts (see *Management*)

Key Question
Using the relative distances of the planets, how can we make a model solar system in the class or on the playground ?

Background Information
    Astronomers use astronomical units to measure distances that are too small to be measured in light years. The distance of each planet from the sun is provided on the chart for the activity *Can You Planet?* Students can refer to that chart or the teacher can provide it. To find the astronomical unit, students use a comparative ratio. By simply dividing the distances in millions of kilometers, students can work with smaller numbers. After they have determined relative distances, they can let the earth equal any distance they wish and simply multiply that by the relative distance to create their model. Distances given are the average mean distance from a planet to the earth or the sun. Using the distance of

earth from the sun as one centimeter, students can space the planets on a piece of 12" x 18" paper. Using 0.5 meter to represent earth's distance from the sun, students can measure relative distances on most school playgrounds. The following chart shows relative distances and sizes to scale.

Planet	Model Scale (mm)	Distance Scale (m)
Mercury	1	12
Venus	2	22
Earth	2	30
Mars	1	46
Jupiter	28	155
Saturn	26	285
Uranus	10	574
Neptune	9	899
Pluto	1	1191

Management
1. This activity will probably take two class periods; one period to complete the computation and another to actually measure the distances.
2. Students can work in pairs or small groups to do this activity.
3. Students need to have some idea of how a ratio works before completing the activity.
4. For worksheet one, let the distance for earth equal one centimeter. Students can cut circles to represent the planets or use the following seeds and nuts. Radish seeds: Mercury and Pluto, split pea: Mars, dried pea: Earth and Venus, lima beans: Uranus and Neptune, and walnuts: Jupiter and Saturn. This scale will fit on a 12" x 18" paper.
5. Relative size can be determined using the worksheet in the following lesson, *Size It Up*.
6. For worksheet two, let a building or wall represent the location of the sun. The distance of the earth may be any amount you decide and depends on the size of your playground. One way to determine this is to have students use metric tapes or a trundle wheel to measure the farthest distance on the playground. From that measurement, they can decide what value they can give to Earth so all the planets will fit.

Procedure
1. Students fill in the distances from the sun for each planet.
2. Students divide distances by 150. Answers should be rounded to the nearest tenth.

3. Using those answers as relative distances, students make a model solar system in the classroom by measuring one centimeter from the end of a 12" x 18" piece of paper and using circles or seeds to represent the planets.

4. Have students use their predetermined measurements to construct a model solar system on the playground.

Discussion

1. What do you notice about the distances from the sun to the inner planets compared with the distances to the outer planets?

2. What observations did you make while looking at the playground model?

Extension

If space permits in either the classroom or outside, choose a central location for the sun and place the planets the relative distance away. This is more realistic since the planets are not lined up in a straight line but rather in different places in their orbits.

*From J. Abruscato et al. **Holt Science** [Grade 5 Pupil Book] (New York: Holt, Rinehart and Winston, 1986). p. 323.

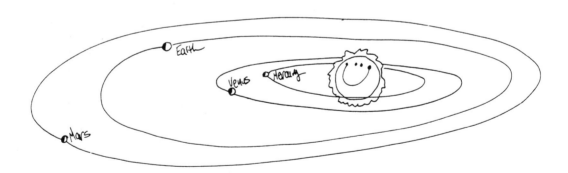

Spacing Out the System

Astronomical Unit

Astronomers have chosen a unit to measure distances in space called the astronomical unit. The length of an astronomical unit is the average distance of the earth from the sun. The distance is about 93,000,000 miles or 150,000,000 kilometers. The exact figure is not as important to us as the ratio or relative distance of the planets from the sun. Using astronomical units, those relative distances stay the same whether we use miles or kilometers.

Using 150,000,000 kilometers as one astronomical unit, you can create a model solar system in your classroom or on the playground.

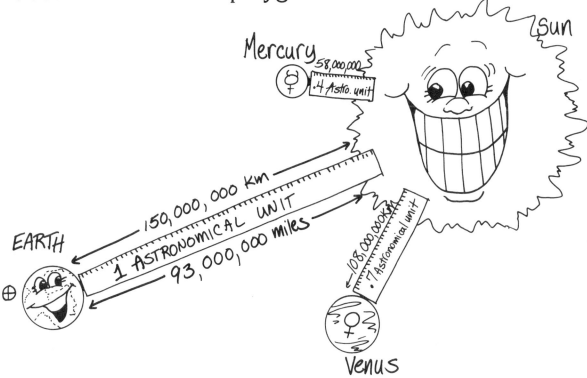

Spacing Out the System

Orbital Distance

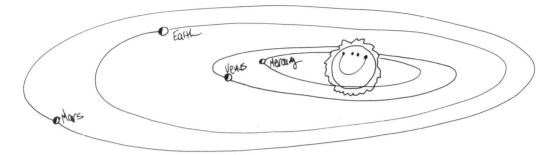

The planets travel in elliptical rather than true circular obrits as they make their way around the sun. This means that they are sometimes closer and sometimes farther away. The distances we are using are called the "mean average". This means the average between a planet's farthest point from the sun or earth and its nearest point. The maximum, minimum, and mean average distances for Earth, Uranus, Neptune, and Pluto are listed below.

	Earth	Uranus	Neptune	Pluto
Maximum distance from sun in millions of kilometers	152.1	3,004	4,537	7,375
Minimum distance from sun in millions of kilometers	147.1	2,735	4,456	4,425
Mean distance from sun in millions of kilometers	150	2,870	4,497	5,900

Pluto has a particularly elongated orbit and at its minimum distance is actually closer to the sun than Neptune.

Spacing Out the System

In order to create a model of the solar system that is accurate in terms of distance you use the astronomical unit, which is the average distance of the earth from the sun, or 150,000,000 kilometers. The distance of the earth from the sun is then equal to one unit. By creating a ratio for each of the other planets, you can determine their relative distances. Here is an example using the planet Mercury.

Distance from the sun in millions of kilometers   Relative Distance

MERCURY $\dfrac{58}{150}$ $=$ $\dfrac{N}{1}$
EARTH

Cross multiply and you find that 150N equals 58. Divide both sides by 150 and you have the relative distance of Mercury from the sun.

Complete the chart below. Round your final answer to the nearest tenth. Round the planets' distances to the nearest million kilometers.

PLANET	Distance in millions of Kilometers	÷ 150 = Relative Distance	Rounded to Nearest Tenth
MERCURY		÷ 150 =	
VENUS		÷ 150 =	
EARTH		÷ 150 =	
MARS		÷ 150 =	
JUPITER		÷ 150 =	
SATURN		÷ 150 =	
URANUS		÷ 150 =	
NEPTUNE		÷ 150 =	
PLUTO		÷ 150 =	

Spacing Out the System

(page 2)

Use the relative distances from the previous page to complete the table below for creating a model solar system for the classroom and playground. Use this information to construct one or both models. Start at one end of a bulletin board or playground and label the sun. Use the chart below and measure to show the relative distances. In the classroom you can also use objects or circles of relative size. On the playground, have a person hold a sign for each planet and stand the measured distance apart. Take turns observing from a distance.

Classroom : Let Earth equal 1 centimeter

Playground : Let Earth equal .5 meter

PLANET		CLASSROOM	PLAYGROUND
MERCURY	☿		
VENUS	♀		
EARTH	⊕		
MARS	♂		
JUPITER	♃		
SATURN	♄		
URANUS	♅		
NEPTUNE	♆		
PLUTO	♇		

Topic Area
Planets

Introductory Statement
Students will determine the relative sizes of the planets in order to construct a model solar system.

Math
Using computation
Rounding
Estimating
Problem solving
Using rational numbers
    decimals
Using geometry

Science
Astronomy
    planets

Math/Science Processes
Recording data
Interpreting data
Predicting and inferring
Making and testing hypotheses
Applying and generalizing

Materials
Calculators
Metric rulers and tapes
Construction paper
Pencils
Clay
Compasses

Key Question
How can we make a model solar system that will show the relative sizes of the planets?

Background Information
    To make a scale model of the solar system, students must give the diameter of the earth a value such as one centimeter and use comparative ratios to determine the relative sizes of the rest of the planets. The diameter of each planet is provided in the chart for the activity *Can You Planet?* Students can refer to that chart, or the teacher can provide the information. Directions for set-ting up the ratio are on the student page. After they have determined relative sizes of the planets, the students are to construct clay balls–also of relative sizes–to use in their model solar system. On worksheet two, students are given diameter lines on which to form these balls. They may then construct larger circles from construction paper, using a larger number (such as ten) for the earth's diameter.

Management
1. This activity may take two class periods, one period to complete the computations and another to actually construct the circles.
2. Students can work in pairs or small groups to do this activity.
3. Students need to have some knowledge of ratios before completing the activity.
4. You can use any number to equal the diameter of earth. *One* was selected to facilitate the formation of the clay balls.
5. Larger circles can be constructed from paper by determining the radius of each one and using a compass to draw it.
6. In constructing the paper models, students need to divide the diameter by two to find the radius of each planet.

Procedure
1. Students fill in the diameter for each planet.
2. Students divide diameters by 12,800, the earth's diameter.
3. Answers should be rounded to the nearest tenth.
4. Using those answers as relative diameters, students make a model solar system in the classroom by constructing clay spheres and/or construction paper circles and placing them relative distances apart.

Discussion
1. What do you notice about the sizes of the various planets?
2. Why was the radius used to construct the paper planets?

Extensions
Once students have constructed the circles, they can experiment to see how many earths it would take to cover Jupiter, Saturn, etc.

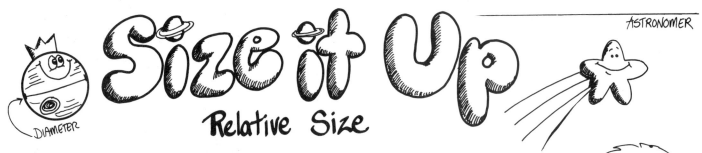

Size it Up
Relative Size

Relative size can be determined in much the same way as relative distance. Give the diameter of earth a value of 1. By creating a ratio, you can obtain the relative size diameter for each planet in the solar system. You can then use that relative size to make your own solar system model by setting up a ratio for each of the planets. Here is a sample using Mercury:

$$\frac{\text{MERCURY'S DIAMETER}}{\text{EARTH'S DIAMETER}} : \frac{4900}{12,800} = \frac{N}{1}$$

Cross multiply and you get the equation $4900 = 12,800\,N$. By dividing both sides by 12,800 you obtain the relative diameter for Mercury. Complete the chart below for all the planets.

Planet	Diameter	÷ (EARTH'S DIAMETER) 12,800	= Relative Diameter
Mercury		÷ 12,800 =	
Venus		÷ 12,800 =	
Earth	12,800	÷ 12,800 =	1
Mars		÷ 12,800 =	
Jupiter		÷ 12,800 =	
Saturn		÷ 12,800 =	
Uranus		÷ 12,800 =	
Neptune		÷ 12,800 =	
Pluto		÷ 12,800 =	

Size it Up

Solar System Scale Models

— Mercury

— Venus

Earth —

— Mars

1. Make a scale model of the solar system out of clay. The relative diameter for each planet is drawn on the page for you. Form balls of clay with diameters to match. Put the planets in order on your desk.

_____ Jupiter

DIAMETER

Saturn _____

_____ Uranus

2. Make a larger model of the solar system from paper. Do the computations then use a compass to construct the circles. Color and post.

_____ Neptune

.. Pluto

Planet	Relative Diameter	Scale Diameter (x 10)	Radius (÷2)
Mercury	.4		
Venus	.9		
Earth	1	10cm	5cm
Mars	.5		
Jupiter	11.2		
Saturn	9.4		
Uranus	4.0		
Neptune	3.9		
Pluto	.2		

Planetary Scavenger Hunt

Topic Area
Planets

Introductory Statement
Students will use a marble to represent the size of the earth and try to find other spherical objects of relative sizes to represent the rest of the planets.

Math
Using computation
Rounding
Estimating
Measuring diameters
Problem solving
Using decimals

Science
Astronomy
    planets

Math/Science Processes
Recording data
Interpreting data
Predicting and inferring
Making and testing hypotheses
Applying and generalizing

Materials
Pencils
Calculators
Metric rulers and tapes
Books
Balls, marbles, and other spherical objects

Key Question
What everyday objects can we use to represent the relative sizes of the earth and the other planets?

Background Information
    To make a scale model of the solar system using spherical objects, students must first have an object such as a marble to represent earth. They then measure the object to determine the constant factor. By multiplying the relative diameters of the other planets by this constant, they determine the diameters their other objects must have. They then locate objects (seeds of various sizes, a variety of marbles, rubber balls, tennis balls, and larger playground balls) to represent the other planets.

Management
1. This activity may be done over an extended period of time as students search for objects. Several objects can be provided in a classroom setting or students can do this as an out-of-class project and share objects they have found.
2. Students should work in pairs or small groups to do this activity.
3. You can use any object to equal the diameter of earth. A marble was selected because both larger and smaller spheres would be relatively easy to locate.
4. Students determine the diameter of a marble by placing it between two rulers and measuring the distance across as shown. One student holds the two rulers upright against the object while the other student measures the distance between the rulers.
5. Students need to be reminded that all measured numbers are approximate and that they may not find spheres that are exactly equal to a planet's relative diameter.

Procedure
1. Students measure the diameter of the marble to represent Earth. (This number is then recorded for Earth in both the *needed* and *actual* columns.)
2. Students multiply each planet's relative diameter by the diameter of the marble to determine the needed diameter and record those numbers on the chart.
3. Students measure other spherical objects such as balls, seeds, fruit, etc. to find objects with approximate diameters equal to those of the other planets.
4. Record the names of those objects and their diameters, and subtract to find the differences.

Discussion
1. What do you notice about the sizes of the various planets?
2. Did everyone choose the same object to represent a particular planet?

Extensions
    Students could start with a large object like a beach ball representing Jupiter and locate other objects relative to that.

Planetary Scavenger Hunt

Use a marble to represent earth. Measure its diameter and record. That measurement is the constant factor. Multiply each planet's relative diameter by the constant to determine the needed diameter. Scavenge for spheres with appropriate diameters to represent the planets. Measure, record, and find the difference.

	Diameter in Km	Relative Diameter	Objects:	Needed Diameter	Actual Diameter	Difference
Mercury	4,900	.4	_____			
Venus	12,100	.9	_____			
Earth	12,800	1	marble			
Mars	6,800	.5	_____			
Jupiter	143,000	11.2	_____			
Saturn	120,600	9.4	_____			
Uranus	51,100	4.0	_____			
Neptune	49,500	3.9	_____			
Pluto	2,300	.2	_____			

Score: ___

30

EXTRATERRESTRIAL EXCURSIONS

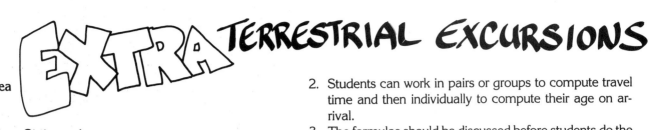

Topic Area
Planets

Introductory Statement
Travel time to the moon and the planets will be computed so that students can determine their ages after making imaginery excursions.

Math
Using computation
Rounding
Estimating
Problem solving
Using rational numbers
   decimals
Using calculators

Science
Astronomy
   planets

Math/Science Processes
Recording data
Interpreting data
Predicting and inferring
Making and testing hypotheses
Applying and generalizing

Material
Calculators

Key Question
Traveling at a speed of 40,000 kilometers per hour, how old would you be upon your arrival at the moon and each planet?

Background Information
   The distance to the moon and each planet (in kilometers) is listed on the student worksheet. (If a teacher prefers, these distances can be researched by the students.) The speed of 40,000 kilometers per hour was determined by the speed of space travel we would be capable of today. Obviously there would be more to interplanetary travel than how long it would take, and students may bring up all those problems.

   Since the answers to the first three computations should be rounded, rounding strategies should be taught prior to this activity. The last computation (converting months to years) should be done without a calculator, as the remainder will tell students the number of months. This serves as a good example of a situation in which computing with a calculator won't work. The final activity sheet, *Special Delivery*, gives students the opportunity to use the information in a problem-solving format.

Management
1. Time for this activity will vary depending on the students' math abilities and whether or not calculators are used.

2. Students can work in pairs or groups to compute travel time and then individually to compute their age on arrival.
3. The formulas should be discussed before students do the worksheet. The formula *rate x time = distance* is an important one which students can use in a variety of situations. We use it as a division formula solving for time.
4. Teaching the process of crossing through an equal number of zeroes before dividing is very helpful. If students are dividing without calculators, this means they only need to divide by 4.
5. When doing *Special Delivery*, students have to be reminded that a visit to any planet is not complete until they return to earth.

Procedure
1. On *Extraterrestrial Excursions*, students will record their ages in years and months.
2. Students will predict how long it will take to travel to the moon and each of the planets; then they will record their predicted ages on arrival.
3. Students will use the formulas to compute travel time to the moon and each planet.
   - Compute hours of travel time by dividing the distance from Earth by the speed of 40,000 kilometers per hour. Round to the nearest hour.
   - Compute the days traveled by dividing the hours by 24 and round to the nearest day.
   - Compute travel time in months by dividing days by 30 and rounding to the nearest month.
   - Compute years traveled by dividing months by 12 without using a calculator. The remainder is used to record the number of years and months.
4. By adding that amount of time to their ages, students will arrive at their actual ages at the time of arrival.
5. Students record their actual arrival ages in the last column on the worksheet.
6. Students use the information about travel time to answer the questions on *Special Delivery*.
7. Students create their own mystery trips for their classmates to answer.

Discussion
1. How did your predictions compare to the actual age you would be?
2. Were you surprised by how long or short a time it would take for interplanetary travel?

Extensions
1. Have students compute how long it would take them to travel to a given planet and return.
2. Ask students to compute the arrival ages for other family members.
3. Students can list supplies needed for a lengthy voyage.
4. Have students write an imaginary journal of their voyage.

Travel Time

The great distances in space are sometimes difficult to comprehend. If we look at the time it would take to travel to the moon and the planets by walking, by car, or by jet plane, we can begin to understand what a great undertaking interplanetary travel would be.

TIME IN YEARS FROM EARTH

Planetary Body	Walking 2.5/mph 3.6/Kmph	Car 55mph 80 Kmph	Jet 990 mph 1436 Km ph
Moon	11	.6	.03
Mercury	2588	133	7
Venus	1175	61	3
Mars	2222	113	6
Jupiter	17,843	909	46
Saturn	36,421	1848	92
Uranus	76,894	3935	194
Neptune	123,579	6289	313
Pluto	162,622	8378	410

EXTRA TERRESTRIAL EXCURSIONS

SPEED LIMIT
40,000 Km per hr

SPACE VOYAGER

Name: _____

Age Today

YEARS: _____ MONTHS: _____

How old will you be?

AVERAGE DISTANCE FROM EARTH		HOURS	DAYS	MONTHS	YEARS		ARRIVAL AGE	
		Distance / 40,000 (to nearest hour)	Hours / 24 (to nearest day)	Days / 30 (to nearest month)	Month / 12		Years + your Age	
					Years	Months	Years	Months
384,000 Km	Moon							
92,000,000 Km	Mercury							
41,000,000 Km	Venus							
78,000,000 Km	Mars							
629,000,000 Km	Jupiter							
1,227,000,000 Km	Saturn							
2,721,000,000 Km	Uranus							
4,347,000,000	Neptune							
5,750,000,000	Pluto							

EXTRA TERRESTRIAL EXCURSIONS

SPECIAL DELIVERY

Imagine that you work for the Solar Systems Delivery Service. You need to determine the time necessary to make certain deliveries and return to Earth. The planets are not lined up in a straight line in their orbits around the sun. You must always return to Earth for refueling between planets.

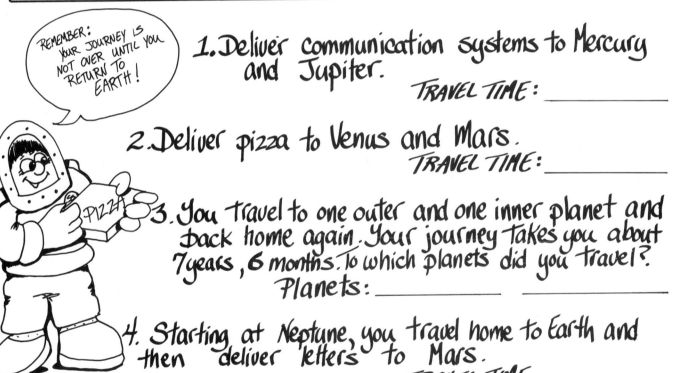

REMEMBER: YOUR JOURNEY IS NOT OVER UNTIL YOU RETURN TO EARTH!

1. Deliver communication systems to Mercury and Jupiter.

TRAVEL TIME: _____

2. Deliver pizza to Venus and Mars.

TRAVEL TIME: _____

3. You travel to one outer and one inner planet and back home again. Your journey takes you about 7 years, 6 months. To which planets did you travel?

Planets: _____ _____

4. Starting at Neptune, you travel home to Earth and then deliver letters to Mars.

TRAVEL TIME: _____

5. Design a "Mystery" trip to two of the planets. Remember to always stop at the Earth between planets. How long would your mystery trip take?

TRAVEL TIME: _____

Exchange "Mystery" trips with another student and solve.

How Long Does it Take to Say..... HELLO?

Topic Area
Planets

Introductory Statement
Students will compute the time it would take for a message to reach the moon and the planets.

Math
Using computation
Rounding
Estimating
Problem solving
Applying formulas
Using calculators

Science
Astronomy
    planets

Math/Science Processes
Recording data
Interpreting data
Predicting and inferring
Making and testing hypotheses
Applying and generalizing

Materials
Calculators

Key Question
How long would it take for someone on the moon or one of the planets to hear you say "hello?"

Background Information
    The distance to the moon and each planet in kilometers is listed on the student worksheet. (If the teacher prefers, these distances can be researched by the students prior to doing the activity.) Because radio waves travel at the speed of light, that is the rate used for transmission. The actual speed of light is 299,739 kilometers per second. It is rounded to 300,000 for ease in calculation since the answers should be rounded. Rounding strategies

should be taught prior to this activity. Numbers may be rounded to the nearest tenth or whole number. The last computation, converting minutes to hours, should be done without a calculator, as the remainder will tell them the number of minutes.

Management
1. Time for this activity will vary depending on the students' math abilities and whether calculators are used.
2. Students can work in pairs or groups to do the computations.
3. The formula should be discussed before students do the worksheet. The formula, *rate x time = distance*, is an important one which students can use in a variety of situations. We used it as a division formula solving for time.
4. Teaching the process of crossing out an equal number of zeroes before dividing makes the process much easier as students then need only to divide by 3. By doing this, students are actually first dividing both numbers by 100,000.

Procedure
1. Students will use the formula on the worksheet to compute the time for a radio message to reach the moon and each planet.
    *   Compute the number of seconds by dividing the distance from earth by the speed of light. Round to the nearest whole number.
    *   Compute the number of minutes by dividing the seconds by 60; then round to the nearest whole number.
    *   Compute time in hours and minutes by dividing minutes by 60. This time, the remainder is used to determine the minutes.

Discussion
1. What do you notice about the differences in amount of time it takes to communicate with the inner and outer planets?
2. What does that tell you about the distances to those planets?

How Long Does it Take. to Say..... HELLO?

Although travel to the far reaches of space is a thing of the future, space communication is not. Exploratory Space Probes, such as Voyager 2, send and receive messages from the very edges of our solar system. Radio waves travel at the speed of light, 299,739 kilometers per second. Use the formulas below to compute how long it would take for your "Hello" to reach the moon and each of the planets.

Destination of Message	Average Distance from Earth in km	Seconds (Distance/rate) (÷300,000)	Minutes (seconds/60) (÷60)	Hours (minute/60) (÷60)
Moon	384,000			
Mercury	92,000,000			
Venus	41,000,000			
Mars	78,000,000			
Jupiter	629,000,000			
Saturn	1,277,000,000			
Uranus	2,721,000,000			
Neptune	4,347,000,000			
Pluto	5,750,000,000			

36

MESSAGE

Topic Area
Planets

Introductory Statement
Students will compute the time it would take for a series of messages to go back and forth between the moon and the planets.

Math
Using computation
Rounding
Estimating
Problem solving

Science
Astronomy
    planets

Math/Science Processes
Recording data
Interpreting data
Predicting and inferring
Making and testing hypotheses
Applying and generalizing

Material
Calculators

Key Question
How long would it take to send a series of communications to the moon or one of the planets?

Background Information
   Students will have computed the time for a one way transmission in the activity *How Long Does it Take to Say Hello?* Now they will use those calculations to compute the time necessary to complete a series of two-way communications. You may use the six-sentence script which is provided, or have students create their own scripts of varying lengths. It works best if students multiply the time for a one-way transmission in minutes (seconds for the moon) by the number of transmissions made. They will then divide any answers over 60 minutes in length by 60 to compute hours and minutes to determine at what time and day they will complete their transmissions.

Management
1. Time for this activity will vary depending on the students' math abilities and whether calculators are used. It will also depend on whether students write their own transmission scripts and take the time to actually try them.
2. Students compute by adding the time of the total transmission to the day and time they began.
3. Students can work in pairs or cooperative groups.
4. Students need to use their answers for a one-way transmission from *How Long Does it Take to Say Hello?*
5. Students then answer the question, "If you began transmitting at 8:00 am Tuesday, what day and time would you finish?"

Procedure
1. Students will use the six-sentence transmission script or write their own.
2. Using the time to complete a one-way transmission in minutes, students will determine the time it would take to complete a two-way transmission of the entire script. This is done by multiplying the time for a one-way transmission by the number of transmissions.
3. If that answer is over 60 minutes, it should be divided by 60 to give the answer in hours and minutes. This will be true for the planets Jupiter through Pluto.
4. Have students compute the day and time their transmission would be complete.

Discussion
1. Between which two planets did you see a change from time in minutes to hours?
2. What is the first and second set of planets called? [inner and outer planets]
3. What lies between these two sets of planets? [the asteroid belt]

SPACE TALK

MESSAGE

You need to send the following important message to Space Bases on the moon and the planets and to receive their responses. Use the transmission time from "How Long Does It Take to Say Hello?" to determine how long each set of transmissions will take.

1. Earth to _____. Do you read me?

2. _____ to Earth. You're coming in loud and clear.

3. All Space Bases must tune in to Channel Z8 on Friday, 9:00 A.M. Solar Standard Time.

4. What's so important?

5. The President of the Galactic Federation will be speaking.

6. Roger, Earth, we'll be listening. This is _____ over and out.

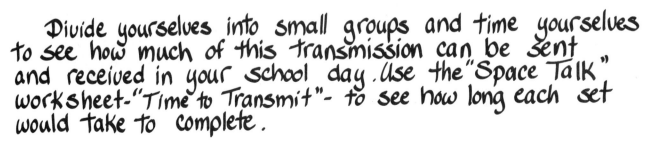

Divide yourselves into small groups and time yourselves to see how much of this transmission can be sent and received in your school day. Use the "Space Talk" worksheet-"Time to Transmit"- to see how long each set would take to complete.

Write your own set of messages sent and received. Determine how long it would take to complete them.

SPACE TALK

TIME TO TRANSMIT......

Use the data from "How Long Does It Take to Say Hello?" to compute the total transmission time for your message.

If you began transmitting on Tuesday at 8:00 A.M., what day and time would you finish.

	One Way Transmission Time from Earth		Number of Transmissions		Total Transmission Time
Moon		×		=	minute : seconds :
Mercury					hours : minutes :
Venus					hours : minutes :
Mars					hours : minutes :
Jupiter					hours : minutes :
Saturn					hours : minutes :
Uranus					hours : minutes :
Neptune					hours : minutes :
Pluto					hours : minutes :

Time at Completed Transmission (Day) (Time)

Weight in Space

Topic Area
Planets

Introductory Statement
Students will determine their weight on the moon and the other planets.

Math
Using computation
Using rational numbers
   Rounding
Graphing
Estimating

Science
Astronomy
   planets

Math/Science Processes
Classifying
Comparing data
Interpreting data
Predicting and inferring
Applying and generalizing

Materials
Calculators

Key Questions
What do you think you would weigh on the moon?...on the planet _____?

Background Information
   The gravity of an object is related to its mass and density. The more mass an object has, the stronger its pull of gravity. Gravitational pull weakens with distance. The **mean** densities of the outer planets are less than Earth. (Their interior densities, however, are far greater.) Saturn actually has a mean density less than water.

   The surface gravity of earth is considered as *one* and the moon and the other planets are considered as a fraction of that. Each student will multiply the estimated surface gravity for the specific planets times his or her weight in either pounds (or kilograms) to determine their weight on the various planets. Information about the surface gravity of some planets varies. The figure 0.03 for Pluto is a scientific estimate. Students should be reminded that events such as the Voyager II flyby of Neptune in 1989 are constantly updating our information about space.

Management
1. This activity will take about 30-40 minutes.
2. Students can either be weighed in class or bring their recorded weight from home.
3. If students are sensitive about their weights, they could use a weight they would like to be or the weight of an object in the classroom.
4. Students should round their weight to the nearest pound or kilogram and record this under *Actual Weight* on the first activity sheet.
5. Students subtract to find how much more or less they would weigh on a planetary body than on Earth and record this in the difference column on the first page.
6. Students will graph their weights on the various planets using the third worksheet.

Discussion
1. What would be some of the effects of the different weights?
2. What causes the differences in surface gravity?
3. If Uranus is larger than the earth, why is its surface gravity less?
4. What would it be like for you on the moon?...on Jupiter?...on the other planets?

Extensions
1. Have students research the mass and density of the various planets. What effect does this have on the surface gravity?
2. If a computer is available, students might use a program such as *Planetarium on Computer* by Focus Media Inc. which explores the concept of mass as well as orbit and location.
3. Use the provided Basic program to determine weights on the planets.

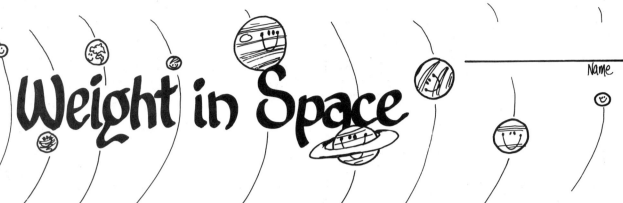

Weight in Space

Gravity is an invisible force that pulls on things. The pull of earth's gravity is what gives us weight. The size, mass, and density of a planet or moon determines its gravitational pull. We consider the surface gravity of the earth to be 1. Look at the chart of surface gravities of the moon and other planets and predict what you think your weight would be on each of them.

My weight on earth is _____ .

	Estimated Surface Gravity	Predicted Weight	Actual Weight	Difference
Moon	.16			
Mercury	.39			
Venus	.91			
Mars	.38			
Jupiter	2.60			
Saturn	1.07			
Uranus	.90			
Neptune	1.15			
Pluto	.03			

On which planet would you weigh the least? _____

On which planets would you weigh more than on the earth? _____

On which planets would you weigh nearly the same as on earth? _____

Weight in Space-2

To find your actual weight on the moon and the planets, you must multiply your weight on earth by the surface gravity of that body. Find your weight on the moon first and then follow the formula to complete the chart below.

Use the surface gravities from the chart on the previous page. Round your answer to the nearest whole number.

The surface gravity on the moon is one sixth or .16 that of earth.

Planetary Body	My Weight on Earth ✗	Surface Gravity =	My weight on Planetary Body
Moon			
Mercury			
Venus			
Mars			
Jupiter			
Saturn			
Uranus			
Neptune			
Pluto			

For which planet was your prediction the closest? _____

For which planet was your prediction the most different? _____

On which planet was your weight closest to that on earth? _____

Weight in Space Graph

Weight

300+
300
290
280
270
260
250
240
230
220
210
200
190
180
170
160
150
140
130
120
110
100
90
80
70
60
50
40
30
20
10

Moon Mercury Venus Earth Mars Jupiter Saturn Uranus Neptune Pluto

43

YOUR WEIGHT
IN SPACE

```
10      REM : THIS PROGRAM CALCULATES YOUR WEIGHT ON OTHER PLANETS
20      PRINT " THIS PROGRAM WILL TELL YOU HOW MUCH YOU WILL WEIGH ON OTHER PLANETS
25      HOME
30      INPUT "WHAT IS YOUR WEIGHT ON EARTH?";A
40      INPUT "WHAT PLANET ARE YOU ON?";Z$
45      PRINT
50      IF Z$ = "MERCURY" GOTO 120
60      IF Z$ = "VENUS" GOTO 150
70      IF Z$ = "MARS" GOTO 180
80      IF Z$ = "JUPITER" GOTO 210
90      IF Z$ = "SATURN" GOTO 240
100     IF Z$ = "URANUS" GOTO 270
110     IF Z$ = "NEPTUNE" GOTO 300
115     IF Z$ = "PLUTO" GOTO 330
120     LET ME = A * .16
130     PRINT "ON MERCURY YOU WOULD WEIGH ";ME
135     PRINT
140     GOTO 40
150     LET V = A * .91
160     PRINT "ON VENUS YOU WOULD WEIGH ";V
165     PRINT
170     GOTO 40
180     LET MA = A * .38
190     PRINT "ON MARS YOU WOULD WEIGH ";MA
195     PRINT
200     GOTO 40
210     LET J = A * 2.6
220     PRINT "ON JUPITER YOU WOULD WEIGH ";J
225     PRINT
230     GOTO 40
240     LET S = A * 1.07
250     PRINT "ON SATURN YOU WOULD WEIGH ";S
255     PRINT
260     GOTO 40
270     LET V = U * .90
280     PRINT "ON URANUS YOU WOULD WEIGH ";U
285     PRINT
290     GOTO 40
300     LET N = A * 1.15
310     PRINT "ON NEPTUNE YOU WOULD WEIGH ";N
315     PRINT
320     GOTO 40
330     LET P = U * .05
340     PRINT "ON PLUTO YOU WOULD WEIGH ";P
345     PRINT
350     GOTO 40
```

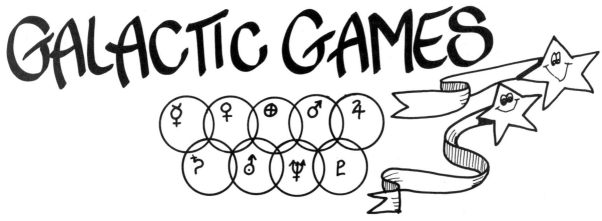

GALACTIC GAMES

Topic Area
Planets

Introductory Statement
Students will compute gravity factors to determine how far and high they could jump and throw on a planetary body.

Math
Using whole number computation
Averaging
Rounding
Measuring
    length
    time
Problem solving

Math/Science Processes
Observing
Measuring
Gathering and recording data
Interpreting data
Applying and generalizing

Materials
Butcher paper
Masking tapes
Ink pad
Paper towels
Measuring tape
Stopwatch
Sponge-like ball
Calculators

Key Question
How far or high can you jump and throw on the moon and the planets?

Background Information
    Gravity is an invisible force that pulls on objects. All the planets in our solar system have a gravitational pull. The gravitational pull of each planet is different because of its mass and density. The surface gravity of Earth is considered to be *one*. Students will use the surface grav-ity of the moon and planets to compute *gravity factors*. By multiplying the gravity factor by any measurable quantity from an activity performed on Earth, they can determine their performance on other planetary bodies.

Management
1. Students work in small groups.
2. Set up four centers around the room: *Quantum Leap, Gravity Defiance, Planetary Pitch*, and *Asteroid Throw*.
3. At the *Quantum Leap* center, mark off a starting place with masking tape so that students can make a standing long jump. Place two or three measuring tapes at this location.
4. At the *Gravity Defiance* center, tape a sheet of butcher paper to the wall at a height you estimate students can reach when they jump up. Leave one tape measure, the ink pad, and paper towels for ink cleanup at this center.
5. At the *Planetary Pitch* center, mark off a starting line with masking tape in an area where students can throw a ball. Leave several measuring tapes, and a sponge-like ball.
6. For *Asteroid Throw*, set up a center outside where students can throw a ball up into the air. Leave a stopwatch, and ball at this center.
7. Prior to the activity, write the rules for the *Galactic Games* (see *Procedure*) on cardstock and place them at the various locations where the events will be held.

Procedure
Activity Sheet 1
1. Students use the first activity sheet to compute the gravity factor for the moon and the planets. Students record which three pairs of planets have gravity factors which are the same.
2. Assign students to various centers. Explain the rules of each event and tell the students that they will make three trials for each event.

Quantum Leap
1. With feet on starting line, long jump as far as possible.
2. Measure distance from starting line to the closest place to the starting line that your body touched.
3. Record distance and repeat two more times.

Gravity Defiance
1. Mark your index finger using the ink pad.
2. Reach as high as you can and mark the paper. This is your *base mark*.
3. Remark your index finger using the ink pad. Jump up and mark as high as you can. This is your *jump mark*.
4. Measure the distance between the *base mark* and the *jump mark*.
6. Enter the information on the worksheet and repeat for two more trials.

Planetary Pitch
1. With feet on the starting line, throw the ball as far as possible.
2. Measure distance from where the ball first hits the ground to the starting line.
3. Record distance on worksheet and repeat two more times.

Asteroid Throw
1. Throw the ball up into the air at the timer's signal.
2. The timer times the ball from the time it leaves your hand until it hits the ground.
3. Record the information and repeat for two more trials.

Discussion
1. On which planetary body would you score the highest?...the lowest?
2. What are some everyday tasks that would be difficult on the moon?...on Jupiter? Explain
3. What are some other earthly events we could measure?
4. On which planetary bodies would your performance be closest to that on earth?
5. Would you be able to win in a competition with your friend if you were on Venus? Explain.

Extensions
1. Have students measure other activities and compute for the planets.
2. Graph the results, comparing the planets.
3. Have students try to perform everyday tasks with weights on their legs or arms.
4. Have the students throw lighter or heavier objects to compare the time and height they reach.

Curriculum Correlation
1. Have students write what it would be like to live on the moon or one of the planets.
2. Have students write what it would be like to play a baseball game on the moon or one of the planets.
3. Read *Matthew Looney's Invasion of Earth*, the story of a young moon boy, by Jerome Beatty.

GALACTIC GAMES

Gravity is an invisible force that pulls on objects. Each of the planets in our solar system has a gravitational pull that is different because of its mass and density. The surface gravity of Earth is considered to be 1. Each planet has a different surface gravity. Athletic events on other planets would have much different outcomes. To find the gravity factor for each of the planets, divide the surface gravity of Earth (1) by the surface gravity of each planet. Find the gravity factor for each planet.

Use this gravity factor to determine how long and how high you can jump and throw on the other planets.

ROUND GRAVITY FACTORS TO THE NEAREST TENTH.

Planetary Body	Gravity on Earth		Surface Gravity	Gravity Factor
Moon	1	÷	.16	=
Mercury	1	÷	.39	=
Venus	1	÷	.91	=
Mars	1	÷	.38	=
Earth	1	÷	1	=
Jupiter	1	÷	2.60	=
Saturn	1	÷	1.07	=
Uranus	1	÷	.90	=
Neptune	1	÷	1.15	=
Pluto	1	÷	.03	=

On which pairs of planets is the gravity factor almost the same?

1. _____ _____
2. _____ _____
3. _____ _____

47

GALACTIC GAMES

Name of Competitor: _____

Name of Team: _____

Flag:

Names of Team
Members:
_____
_____

Compete in each event. Make 3 trials and find the Average.

Asteroid Throw

Trial 1: _____

2: _____

3: _____

Total: _____

Average: _____

Planetary Pitch

Trial 1: _____

2: _____

3: _____

Total: _____

Average: _____

Gravity Defiance

Trial 1: _____

2: _____

3: _____

Total: _____

Average: _____

Quantum Leap

Trial 1: _____

2: _____

3: _____

Total: _____

Average: _____

START

GALACTIC GAMES

Competitor's Name: _____

Team Name: _____

FORMULA: Average × Gravity Factor = Distance

	Moon x 6.3	Mercury & Mars x 2.6	Venus & Uranus x 1.1	Jupiter x .4	Saturn & Neptune x .9	Pluto x 33.3

	Earth Average
Quantum Leap	
Gravity Defiance	
Planetary Pitch	
Asteroid Throw	

Planet Trivia

Topic Area
Planets

Introductory Statement
Students play *Planet Trivia* as a means of reinforcing and reviewing material.

Science
Astronomy
    planets

Math/Science Processes
Problem solving
Applying
Interpreting data

Materials
One set of trivia cards and directions for each 2-9 students
One blank page per student to write additional questions

Key Question
What information do you need to know to play *Planet Trivia*?

Background Information
   Most of the answers can be found in the information provided in this book. A few questions such as, "What star is closest to the earth?" [the sun], are general knowledge questions. Students should be encouraged to write questions of their own that require extra research.

Management
1. Play time will vary depending on whether play is done individually or by teams and the number of players there are.
2. Divide students into groups. Students can play as individuals in groups of two to eight students or as teams of two to four players each.
3. Each group is given a set of cards and a rule sheet.
4. The player or team with the most cards at the end of the playing time wins.

Procedure
1. Each group plays for a given length of time following the rules for individual or team play as provided on the rule sheet.
2. Students use a blank sheet to write additional questions for the game.

Discussion
1. Which questions were the most difficult to answer?
2. Which questions were the easiest to answer?
3. What are some additional questions we can add to the game?

Planet Trivia
Game Rules

Two to eight players for each set of cards, individual or in teams of two to four players each.

INDIVIDUAL PLAY

Deal six cards face down to each player. This is your hand for the first round of Planet Trivia. Set any extra cards aside.

The person to the right of the dealer begins by asking the person on his or her right a question. If the correct answer is given, the player giving the answer takes the card, keeping it separate from his or her hand. If an incorrect answer is given, the person asking the question reads the correct answer and places the card in the discard pile at the center of the table. Play passes to the right until everyone has used their six cards. The player with the most cards at the end of the game is the winner. To play again, shuffle and redeal.

TEAM PLAY

Shuffle the cards and deal each team 16 cards face down. Set remaining cards aside. Teams take turns asking questions of the opposing team. Teams are allowed 20 seconds to confer before giving an answer, but only one answer may be given. When a team answers correctly if keeps the card. If an incorrect answer is given, the correct answer is read and the question is placed in the discard pile. Play continues until both teams use all sixteen cards. The team with the most cards wins.

PLANET TRIVIA CARDS

Q: Which planet is farthest from the sun?

A: Neptune until 1999 then Pluto will be

Q: Which planet has the most moons?

A: Saturn

Q: Which two planets have no moons?

A: Venus & Mercury

Q: Which planet has the shortest year?

A: Mercury

Q: Which planet has the longest period of rotation?

A: Venus ♀

Q: What star is closest to Earth?

A: the Sun

Q: Which planet travels around the sun once every 248 Earth years?

A: Pluto

Q: What is the largest planet in the solar system?

A: Jupiter

Q: Which planet is considered to be Earth's twin in mass and size?

A: Venus ♀

Q: What is the second largest planet in the solar system?

A: Saturn

Q: What is the astronomical term for the distance light travels in a year?

A: a light year

Q: What fraction of your weight would you weigh on the moon?

A: one sixth (1/6)

Q: What planet was discovered in the 20th century?

A: Pluto ♇

Q: Which planet is closest to the Sun?

A: Mercury

Q: Which planet has the largest volcano in the solar system?

A: Mars

Q: What mythological person was the planet closest to the earth named for?

A: Venus – goddess of love

—

PLANET TRIVIA CARDS

Q: Which planet has a surface gravity closest to that on Earth? A: Saturn	Q: Which planet boasts the Great Red Spot? A: Jupiter	Q: What space probe photographed the rings of Uranus? A: Voyager II.	Q: What is the largest satellite orbiting the Earth? A: the Moon
Q: Which planet has the largest mass? A: Jupiter	Q: Which planets did the Mariner spacecraft explore? A: Mercury & Mars	Q: What planet is often referred to as the morning and evening star? A: Venus	Q: What are the solar system's planets named for? A: Ancient gods
Q: On which planet would you weigh the least? A: Pluto	Q: Which planet's day is closest in length to Earth's? A: Mars	Q: Which planet is called the Red Planet? A: Mars	Q: What planet was discovered beyond the orbit of Saturn in 1781? A: Uranus
Q: Which planet has a density less than water? A: Saturn	Q: Which planet has a day that is longer than its period of revolution A: Mercury	Q: Which planet is brightest as seen from Earth? A: Venus	Q: What is the Earth's home Galaxy called? A: The Milky Way

PLANET TRIVIA CARDS

Q: Which planets are larger than Earth?

A: Jupiter, Saturn, Uranus, Neptune

Q: Which planets are smaller than Earth?

A: Mercury, Mars, Pluto, Venus

Q: What are the names of the outer planets?

A: Jupiter, Saturn, Uranus, Neptune, Pluto

Q: What are the names of the inner planets?

A: Mercury, Venus, Earth, Mars

Q: Which planets have seasons, other than Earth?

A: Mars, Uranus, Pluto

Q: How many months does it take for the moon to revolve around the earth?

A: one

Q: Which planet has a moon almost as big as itself?

A: Pluto

Q: How fast can we radio messages through space?

A: the speed of light

Q: What is an astronomical unit equal to?

A: Earth's distance from the sun

Q: What is the name of the unit astronomers use to measure near by space distances?

A: Astronomical unit

Q: Which two planets sometimes switch places in their orbits?

A: Neptune, Pluto

Q: Which planet is sometimes called a double planet?

A: Pluto

Q: What planet is named for the god of the sea and what is its symbol?

A: Neptune, trident

Q: Which planet spins on its side?

A: Uranus

Q: Which planet has "ears"?

A: Saturn

Q: Which planet is surrounded by acid clouds?

A: Venus

PLANET TRIVIA CARDS

Topic Area
Space voice communication and recognition of geometric shapes.

Introductory Statement
The students will experience how space voice communication worked early in the space program, familiarize themselves with geometric shapes, learn to give clear instructions, and practice listening carefully to their peers.

Math
Using geometry and spatial sense
Using rational numbers
     percentages
Using computation

Math/Science Processes
Communicating
Observing
Measuring and comparing
Applying and generalizing

Materials
For each pair of students:
     2 sets geometric shapes (either provided patterns or student constructed shapes)
     2 small zipper-type plastic bags or envelopes
     2 sheets 8 1/2" x 11" paper, plain or construction-type
     scissors or crayons
     optional: compass

For the class:
     optional: overhead projector
     optional: colored plastic shapes for overhead

Key Question
If you were an astronaut in space, how could you repair malfunctioning equipment with instructions coming from mission control?

Background Information
    Early in the space program, it was necessary to rely entirely on voice communication to give and receive instructions. This is still true in some cases. A special skill is involved in being able to give precise and clear instructions, to listen with care, and to follow such instructions accurately.

Management
1. This activity may take two or three days to complete depending upon whether or not students construct the shapes. The teacher has the option of letting the students draw their shapes or having them cut those provided.
2. With younger children, it may be easier to have the shapes already made and placed in the plastic bags or envelopes. If you have the shapes made in advance, start with *Day 2* of the *Procedure*.
3. Each student pair must have two identical sets of shapes, one for the astronaut and the other for the mission control office. Eight different shapes are included in this lesson. Congruent shapes should be colored the same. The emphasis is on recognizing shapes rather than differentiating colors. If the attribute of color is also to be used, then each set of shapes must be produced in several colors.

Procedure
Day 1
1. If you are making your own shapes, have the students follow the directions for construction. Make sure that the partners draw the same-sized shapes and color them the same.
2. Have the student pairs cut out the shapes and place them in plastic bags or envelopes. Each bag should have two of each size, shape, and color.

Day 2
3. Have the student pairs decide who will be the mission control officer and who will be the astronaut.
4. Distribute the bags containing shapes. Have each pair divide the shapes to check that each person has a set of congruent shapes. Provide each pair with two sheets of paper to be used as instrument panels.
5. Explain to the students that when the space program first began, the spacecrafts did not carry television cameras. Mission control and the astronauts communicated without seeing each other, just by voices, so it was very important that the information given was correct and in detail.
6. After the students have their shapes ready, take the students through the following practice with the teacher (or a student who has been briefed) playing the role of the mission control officer. All other students play the role of astronauts. When giving these instructions during this practice session, it may be

helpful to display the shapes on the overhead projector so the students can see if they have placed their shapes correctly. In these instructions, it is assumed all students use the same color configurations.

Astronaut Jane:
Place your rectangular panel in front of you so the longer side of the rectangle is at the bottom. Place the large square in the upper left-hand corner of the instrument panel. (Allow time for others to construct each step.)

Astronaut Jane:
Place the small circle in the middle of the square.

Astronaut Jane:
Place the large rectangle along the right side of the square so its longer side touches the top of the instrument panel.

Astronaut Jane:
Place the large circle so it is tangent to the large rectangle at the mid-point of its base.

Astronaut Jane:
Place the small hexagon in the lower right hand corner of the instrument panel so one side rests on the bottom of the rectangle.

Astronaut Jane:
Place the small ellipse in the center of this large hexagon.

Astronaut Jane:
Place the small rectangle along the top of the hexagon so it touches the right side of the instrument panel.

7. After you have finished giving directions, have the students answer the top part of the activity sheet.
8. Now have the students sit back-to-back with their shapes in front of them. The student who is at mission control will be giving directions to the student who is the astronaut. The first time the astronaut may not ask questions of mission control. When repeating the procedure, the students may ask questions of each other. It may be helpful to have the students say their names when giving directions so that other students don't become confused by listening to another pair.
9. Give the students a time limit of 5 to 10 minutes. At the end of the time limit, have the students check each others work to see how many shapes were correctly placed.
10. Have students fill in their worksheets.

Discussion
1. Is it important to have good communication between mission control and the astronauts? Explain.
2. How do we benefit in our everyday life from the improvements in communication that have been made because of the space program?

DIRECTIONS FOR MAKING GEOMETRIC SHAPES

HEXAGON

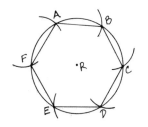

H1 Draw a circle on your paper.
H2 Label the center R.
H3 Choose a point on the circle and label it A.
H4 Use your compass and measure from A to R. Using the distance mark off arcs around the circle starting with point A.
H5 The last arc should intersect point A.
H6 Label each point where the arc and circle intersect B, C, D, E and F.
H7 Connect all points and you will have a Hexagon.

TRIANGLE

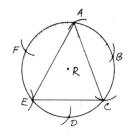

T1 Follow directions for hexagon H1 through H6.
T2 Connect points A, C and E and you will have a Triangle.

SQUARE

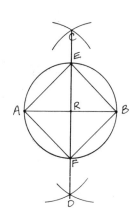

S1 Draw a circle and label the center R.
S2 Draw a horizontal line through the middle of the circle to the other side.
S3 Label the points that intersect the circle A and B.
S4 Using the distance from A to B, place your compass metal point on A and the pencil on B. Now swing your compass so that it makes an arc above and below your circle.
S5 Without changing the compass setting put your metal point on B and the pencil on A. Again make an arc above and below the circle. Label the intersections of the arcs C and D.
S6 Draw a line that goes through point C and D. At the two points where the line intersects the circle, label the first one E and the second one F.
S7 Connect points A, E, B, F. You will have a Square.

OCTAGON

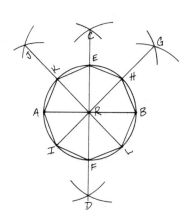

O1 Follow steps S1 through S6 on the square directions.
O2 Place the point of your compass on point B and the pencil on point E and draw an arc.
O3 Keep your compass the same, and put your point on E and the pencil on B. Again, draw an arc. Label this point G where the two lines intersect.
O4 Draw a line that goes through point G and R to the other side of the circle.
O5 At the two points where the line intersects the circle, label the first point H and the second point I.
O6 Repeat steps O2 to O5 of the octagon directions. This time use points A and E. Then draw your two arcs above the circle. Label that point J.
O7 Label the points where the line intersects the circle K and L.
O8 Connect points A, K, E, H, B, L, F and I.

PHONE HOME

Geometric Shapes

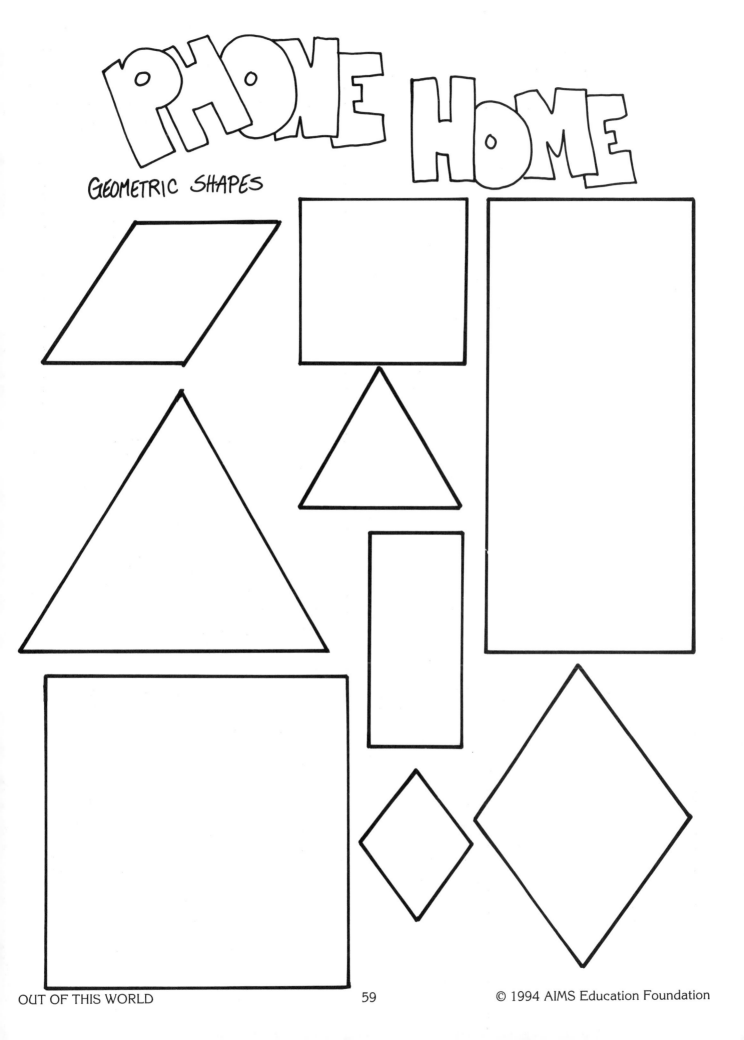

59 © 1994 AIMS Education Foundation

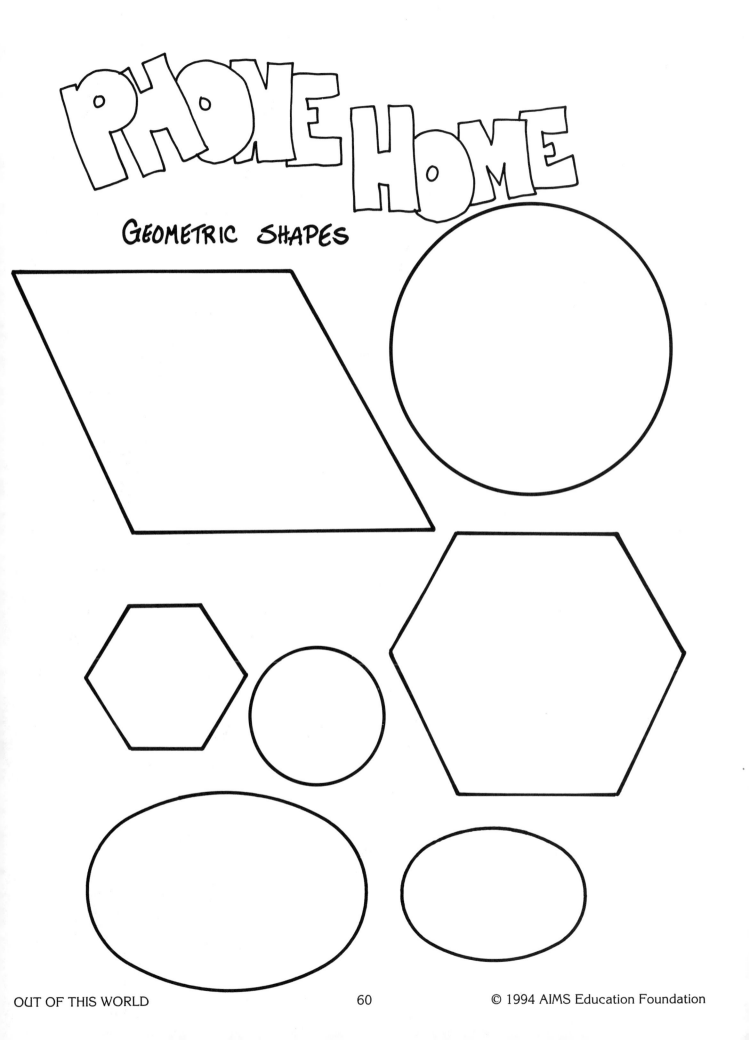

PHONE HOME

Geometric Shapes

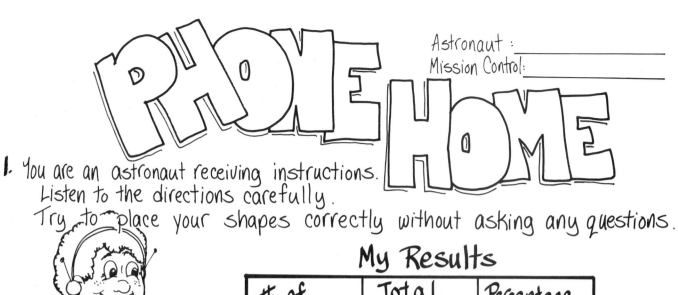

PHONE HOME

Astronaut : _____
Mission Control: _____

1. You are an astronaut receiving instructions.
   Listen to the directions carefully.
   Try to place your shapes correctly without asking any questions.

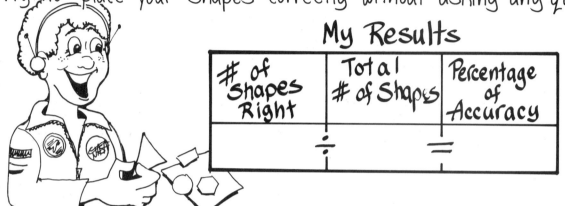

My Results

# of Shapes Right	Total # of Shapes	Percentage of Accuracy
÷	=	

2. Next, work with a partner. Take turns being the astronaut and Mission Control. Listen to your partner's instructions and try to place your shapes correctly <u>without</u> asking questions. Record each person's results as the <u>astronaut.</u>

WITHOUT QUESTIONS

My Results

# of Shapes Correct	Total # of Shapes	Percentage of Accuracy
÷	=	

PARTNER'S Results

# of Shapes Correct	Total # of Shapes	Percentage of Accuracy
÷	=	

3. Try it one more time. This time, you may ask questions when given directions. Record each astronaut's results.

WITH QUESTIONS

My Results

# of Shapes Correct	Total # of Shapes	Percentage of Accuracy
÷	=	

Partner's Results

# of Shapes Correct	Total # of Shapes	Percentage of Accuracy
÷	=	

Astronaut: _____

PHONE HOME

Questions ?

1. Who had the highest percentage of accuracy? _____

2. How many figures did you place correctly?
   Trial 2: _____   Trial 3: _____

3. On a scale of 1 to 10, how hard was it to be Mission Control?

   1———————5———————10

4. On a scale of 1 to 10, how hard was it to be the astronaut?

   1———————5———————10

5. Which of the two was harder for you? _____
   Why? _____

6. On a scale of 1 to 10, how hard was Trial 2? (no communication)

   1———————5———————10

7. On a scale of 1 to 10, how hard was Trial 3? (with communication)

   1———————5———————10

8. Which did you like better, being Mission Control or being the astronaut? Why? _____
   _____

9. What would you do to make communication better between the astronaut and Mission Control? _____
   _____

SPACE★SURVIVAL★AWARD

has been presented to

Astronaut: _____

for outstanding decisions in the face of extreme danger.

Medal
of
Honor

Dated: _____
Signed: _____
Galactic President

SPACE CAPSULE

Topic Area
Time capsule for space

Introductory Statement
Students will determine what items they would send in a time capsule to extraterrestrial life on another planet.

Math
Sorting
Problem solving
Graphing

Math/Science Processes
Collection and recording data
Interpreting data
Generalizing

Materials
Scissors
16 envelopes

Key Question
What would you send to another planet that might best exemplify how we live on the planet Earth?

Management
1. This activity may take one to two days to complete.
2. Reproduce two copies of *Space Capsule* for each student. One is for individual results and the second is for small-group results.
3. Label the 16 envelopes with one each of the listed categories.
4. This activity may be simplified somewhat by suggesting that all events or items emerge from only the twentieth century.
5. Three to four students will work together in groups.

Procedure
1. A suggested introduction may read as follows:
Let us assume that information has been gathered to indicate that extraterrestrial life exists on other planets. Also let us assume that life, with the ability to think, has been found; and now we wish to communicate with them. Because the distance between planets is so great, it would be impossible for us to travel there. Instead, we are going to send a rocket with a time capsule containing 16 well-chosen items that will exemplify life on planet Earth. What should the capsule contain?

2. Each student responds individually by recording on the activity page his or her choice in each of the 16 categories. This page should be put away until later.
3. Students meet in groups to discuss and come to agreement on responses which they record on a second *Space Capsule* page. Record the number of students in each group in the bottom right corner of each category heading. Students cut apart this small group record and place responses by category into appropriately marked envelopes.
4. After all small groups have sorted their responses into respective envelopes, assign groups to sort responses within each envelope to determine the top three responses in each category and the number of students selecting that item. Graph the total number of responses on the graph provided for each category.

Discussion
1. What factors or variables influence ones choice within a category?
2. Discuss how one places value or worth on a given choice.
3. What methods were used to prioritize responses to any one question or category?
4. Why do you think there was so much variation of responses within our class?
5. How did your individual response list compare with your group's?...with the class's?
6. How do you think our responses would compare with students of similar age groups in different geographical areas? How could we find out?

Extensions
1. Compare results in a survey conducted by students of their parents or grandparents. Where are the similarities and the differences?
2. Students predict how their responses would compare with students in similar age groups in different geographical areas.
3. Students will gather data to substantiate their predictions by corresponding with classrooms from other parts of the United States.

SPACE CAPSULE

What would you send to intelligent life on a planet outside _our_ Solar System?

Think about what you would send to represent human life on earth. Write down your responses. Cut apart the strips, place the strips into groups. Tabulate and display your results by graphing.

FAMOUS PERSON:	IMPORTANT INVENTION:
PAST EVENT:	APPLIANCE:
MOVIE:	ELECTRONIC EQUIPMENT:
TELEVISION PROGRAM:	SAMPLE TRANSPORTATION:
BOOK:	SAMPLE SPORT EQUIPMENT:
COMIC STRIP:	GAME:
MUSIC:	TOY:
FOOD:	YOUR CHOICE:

TOP 3 Responses · SPACE CAPSULE - SURVEY RESULTS

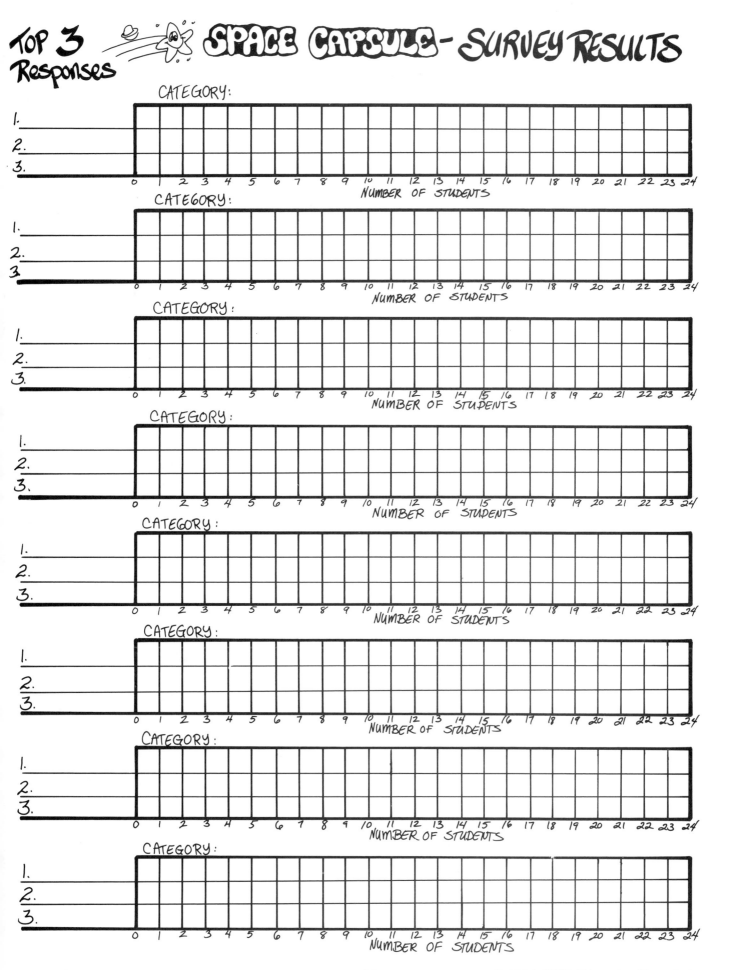

CATEGORY:

1. _____
2. _____
3. _____

0 1 2 3 4 5 6 7 8 9 10 11 12 13 14 15 16 17 18 19 20 21 22 23 24
NUMBER OF STUDENTS

CATEGORY:

1. _____
2. _____
3. _____

0 1 2 3 4 5 6 7 8 9 10 11 12 13 14 15 16 17 18 19 20 21 22 23 24
NUMBER OF STUDENTS

CATEGORY:

1. _____
2. _____
3. _____

0 1 2 3 4 5 6 7 8 9 10 11 12 13 14 15 16 17 18 19 20 21 22 23 24
NUMBER OF STUDENTS

CATEGORY:

1. _____
2. _____
3. _____

0 1 2 3 4 5 6 7 8 9 10 11 12 13 14 15 16 17 18 19 20 21 22 23 24
NUMBER OF STUDENTS

CATEGORY:

1. _____
2. _____
3. _____

0 1 2 3 4 5 6 7 8 9 10 11 12 13 14 15 16 17 18 19 20 21 22 23 24
NUMBER OF STUDENTS

CATEGORY:

1. _____
2. _____
3. _____

0 1 2 3 4 5 6 7 8 9 10 11 12 13 14 15 16 17 18 19 20 21 22 23 24
NUMBER OF STUDENTS

CATEGORY:

1. _____
2. _____
3. _____

0 1 2 3 4 5 6 7 8 9 10 11 12 13 14 15 16 17 18 19 20 21 22 23 24
NUMBER OF STUDENTS

CATEGORY:

1. _____
2. _____
3. _____

0 1 2 3 4 5 6 7 8 9 10 11 12 13 14 15 16 17 18 19 20 21 22 23 24
NUMBER OF STUDENTS

Around the Planets in How Many Days?

Topic Area
Diameter of the planets

Introductory Statement
The students will compare travel time around the equator of each of the planets.

Math
Using whole number operations
   division
   multiplication
Graphing
Rounding
Using formulas
Averaging

Science
Astronomy
   planets

Math/Science Processes
Collection and recording data
Interpreting data
Applying and generalizing

Material
Calculators

Key Question
How much money will you have to spend on fuel to make a trip around the equator of each planet?

Background Information

Planet	Circumference	Diameter	Hours
Mercury	15,390	4,900	159
Venus	38,000	12,100	392
Earth	40,200	12,800	414
Mars	21,350	6,800	220
Jupiter	449,020	143,000	4,629
Saturn	378,680	120,600	3,904
Uranus	160,450	51,100	1,654
Neptune	155,430	49,500	1,602
Pluto	7,220	2,300	74
Total			**13,048**

Planet	Days	Liters of Fuel	Cost
Mercury	7	1,026	$ 410.40
Venus	16	2,533	1,013.20
Earth	17	2,680	1,072.00
Mars	9	1,423	569.20
Jupiter	193	29,935	11,974.00
Saturn	163	25,245	10,098.00
Uranus	69	10,697	4278.80
Neptune	67	10,362	4144.80
Pluto	3	481	192.40
Total	**544**	**84,382**	**$ 33,752.80**

A Land Rover gets 15 kilometers per liter of fuel at a cost of $.40 per liter, and travels at a speed of 97 kilometers per hour.

Management
1. This activity may take 45-90 minutes to complete depending on the arrangement of groups.
2. This activity may be done individually, in small groups, or as a whole class with different students doing the calculations for assigned planets.

Procedure
1. Explain to the students that they will be traveling around the equator of each planet in a Land Rover. The surface texture of each planet will not be taken into consideration. The Land Rover will travel at a speed of 97 kilometers per hour and fuel will cost $.40 per liter.
2. Have the students estimate the number of days it will take to go around the equator. Also have the students estimate the amount of fuel they will need for their journey.
3. Have the students compute the cost of fuel for the trip.
4. Explain to the students how to use the different formulas to answer the questions on the student worksheet. The students will need to round every number to the nearest whole number except the final cost.

Discussion
1. How close was your estimate to what it really costs?
2. How close was your estimate to how many days it will take?
3. Around which planet's equator would you like to travel? Why? Do you think it would be a good investment? Would there be any extra costs? What would they be?

Extensions
1. Have the students design their own Land Rovers. Ask them to explain why they designed them the way they did.
2. Have the students keep logs of their journeys and the adventures that happened.

Around the Planets in How Many Days?

Imagine that it would be possible to travel in a land rover around the equator of each planet in our solar system. Your land rover can travel at a speed of 97 km per hour, gets 15 km per liter of fuel, and the fuel costs $.40 per liter. First estimate the number of days and the cost of the fuel it would take for each planet, then compute to find the actual time and cost.

	Estimation of Days	Estimation of Cost $	Approx. Circumference at Equator	# Hours (C ÷ 97 Kmph)	# Days (Hours ÷ 24)	Fuel Needs (C ÷ 15 = # Liters)	Fuel Costs (# Liters X $.40)
Earth			40,200				
Mercury			15,390				
Venus			38,000				
Mars			21,350				
Jupiter			449,020				
Saturn			378,680				
Uranus			160,450				
Neptune			155,430				
Pluto			7,220				
					Total		Total

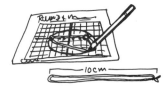

Round and Round

Topic Area
The elliptical orbits of planets

Introductory Statement
Students will construct the shape of planets' orbits in our solar system by drawing ellipses. They will study the effect of several variables on the resulting shape.

Math
Measuring
Constructing ellipses
Examining limits

Science
Astronomy
   planets

Math/Science Processes
Observing
Comparing
Interpreting data
Generalizing

Materials
Pushpins
String
Pencils
Cardboard sheets (8.5" x 11")
Metric rulers

Key Question
What is the shape of a planet's orbit?

Background Information
Planetary orbits are generally elliptical. An ellipse has two foci. In this investigation those two foci are represented by pushpins. If the foci are separated by a distance equal to one-half the length of the closed loop, then the ellipse will be at one limit: a straight line. Note that the loop would then be drawn tight. If the pushpins would have no thickness, the loop would just be a double line. The other limit is reached when the two foci are at one position. In that case, the result would be a circle.

In the first investigation, the length of string forming the loop will be twenty centimeters long and remain as the constant. The manipulated variable will be the distance between the foci, ranging from where both are at the same position (only one pin should be inserted); to where they are separated by ten centimeters (half the distance of the length of the string), in which case a straight line results.

In the second investigation, the length of string will be the manipulated variable and the distance between the foci the constant. The shorter the string, the flatter the ellipse and the longer the string, the more circular will be the ellipse.

Management
1. It is best to do this activity in centers with three to four students in each group.
2. Students can alternate drawing the ellipses.

Procedure
1. Supply each group with the two student worksheets, two pushpins, cardboard backing, string, and metric ruler.
2. Have students tie the string very carefully to produce loops of specified sizes.
3. Demonstrate how to make the construction as shown in the illustration. Direct students to follow the directions found on the top of the activity sheets. The pencil must be held tightly against the string to draw the line.
4. Have students complete both investigations.

Discussion
1. If the length of the loop is held constant, what happens as the distance between the foci increases? When does it become a line?... a circle?
2. If the distance between the foci is held constant, what happens as the length of the loop increases?

Extension
Have the students use different colored construction paper to make the different ellipses described below or others decided upon by the class. Then have them mount the smallest onto the next larger, etc. to create a colorful display. Here is an example of patterns:

Centers	Tacks-Distance	String Length
#1	9cm	25cm
#2	8cm	25cm
#3	12cm	30cm
#4	15cm	35cm
#5	13cm	35cm
#6	11cm	40cm
#7	14cm	40cm
#8	10cm	45cm
#9	12cm	50cm

Round and Round

Name

Tie a string so that its total length is 20cm (10cm doubled up) ⊂══════⊃ ←10cm→.
Place this paper on a piece of cardboard. Push in 2 pins (foci), one at F and F'.
Place your string around the 2 pins and draw your first ellipse. Then,
successively, place your pins at EE', DD', CC', BB', and A (foci are together).

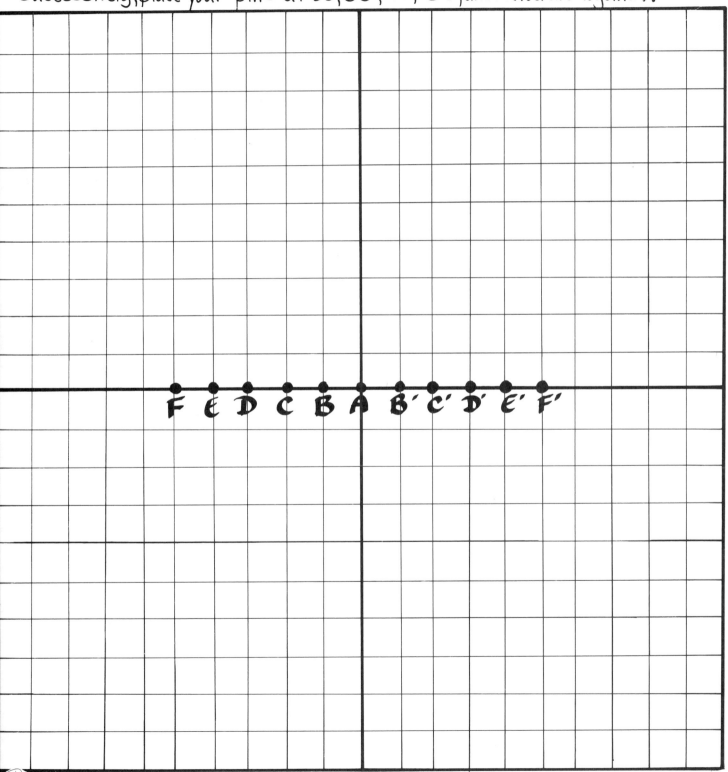

F E D C B A B' C' D' E' F'

Conclusion:

OUT OF THIS WORLD

70

© 1994 AIMS Education Foundation

Round and Round

In this investigation, the variable will be the length of string. Place the pins at E and E'. Draw each ellipse using these foci. Change the length of string each time. Start with 16cm (straight line) and then test 18cm, 20cm, 22cm, and 24cm lengths.

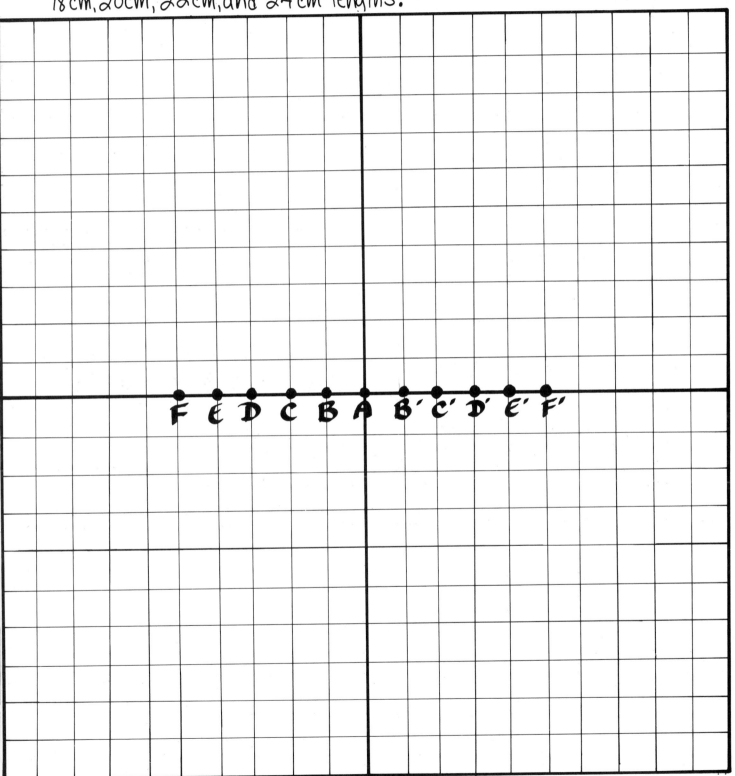

Conclusion:

OUT OF THIS WORLD

© 1994 AIMS Education Foundation

The Moon Shines Bright

Topic Area
The apparent movement of the moon.

Introductory Statement
Students will chart the apparent movement of the moon over a five-hour period and use the information to predict when the moon will rise the following evening.

Math Skills
Using geometry
  measuring angles
Graphing
Using statistics
  mean
Using rational numbers
  percent

Math/Science Processes
Observing
Collecting and recording data
Organizing data
Interpreting data
Comparing
Inferring
Applying

Key Question
What kind of information can we collect in order to predict when the moon will rise tomorrow evening?

Background Information
   The viewed motion of the moon is due to the rotation of the earth. It rotates 15° per hour minus about 0.5° (per hour) which is due to the revolution of the moon around the Earth. Each night the moon will appear a little further to the east amongst the stars as the moon pursues its path around the earth. It is this latter movement which causes it to rise approximately fifty minutes later each night. By measuring the progress of the moon over a five hour period, students should be able to arrive at this approximation and from that predict the rising time of the moon with accuracy. The movement per half-hour is easily detected since the movement per hour is about 14-15 degrees.

Management
1. A clear night at approximately the time of the full moon is necessary for doing this activity.
2. The investigation is most interesting if done before the full moon. Full moon finds the moon rising at the same time the sun is setting. The sun and moon are located in opposite directions as viewed from the earth.

Procedure
1. Divide the class into observation groups. Since this is an evening activity, groups will have to live in the same neighborhood. If some students do not have partners, suggest that their parents help them as the readings are made.
2. Provide each group or individual with the student activity sheets.
3. Have each student construct a *lunometer.*
4. Give students practice in using their lunometers by finding the angle of the sighting of the tops of buildings, trees, etc.
5. Discuss the record sheet for recording the readings.
6. Instruct the students to watch for the moon to rise and carefully record the time. If there are obstructions which block the view to the east, students will also need to measure the angle of sight at which they first see the moon over the obstruction. Observing the time of the moonrise time the evening prior to the activity and adding 50 minutes to that time will predict the time it will rise on the evening of the activity. Students can then be alerted to the approximate time they need to be ready to take readings.
7. Have students take readings every thirty minutes for a four or five hour period. Special permission may be required from parents.
8. Students will then compute the average movement in degrees per half-hour and hour. From this information, they will compute how long it will take to move through 360 degrees.
9. Students will graph the results in half-hour increments. Since the graph will approximate a straight line, students should observe there is a proportion to the amount of elapsed time and the degrees of the elevation of the moon. Therefore, the line can be extended (extrapolated) until it reaches the 90° mark. At that point, one-fourth of the moon's rotation has been completed. By reading the time for that point, students can determine how long it takes for the moon to make .one-fourth of its journey around the earth. Multiplying by four will give the approximate time for the next evening's moonrise.
10. Students will predict the moon's rising time for the four nights following the initial evening of observation. Check the predicted time with the actual time, compute the differences, and find the percentage of error.

Discussion
1. How accurately can we predict moonrise?
2. Which individual or group made the most accurate prediction? Why?
3. Could we predict when the moon will rise ten days from now? How?
4. What causes the moon to rise and to set?

The 🌙 Shines Bright

In the investigation, you will chart the movement of the moon for 5 hours beginning at moonrise. The best time of month is just before full moon. At full moon, the moon rises at the time the sun sets.

Carefully record the time the moon rises and make a measurement of its angle of elevation with your luneometer. This will be zero unless the moon rises behind hills or mountains. Repeat the measurement in every 30 minutes. Observe the timing with care. Enter the information into the table.

One person needs to point the lunometer at the moon and the other take the reading on the scale.

Time	Angle of Elevation	Amount of Change in 30 minutes
Moonrise:		

Total of Change:

Average Change:

The ☺ Shines Bright

Degrees of Elevation

90°
85°
80°
75°
70°
65°
60°
55°
50°
45°
40°
35°
30°
25°
20°
15°
10°
5°
0°

:30 1:00 1:30 2:00 2:30 3:00 3:30 4:00 4:30 5:00 5:30 6:00 6:30 7:00

Amount of Time Elapsed

Graph the Results

How long (in hours and minutes) will it take to have a change of 360 degrees?

Explain: _____

_____
_____
_____

Using the information from your observation predict when the moon will rise in each of the 4 evenings following. Observe the actual rising time and compute your percent of error. Use the time of moonrise observed above for the first date.

Evening:	Date of Observation	Predicted Moonrise Time	Actual Moonrise Time	Difference in Minutes	Per Cent of Error
Initial (full moon)					
First					
Second					
Third					
Fourth					
			Totals:		
			Averages:		

Constructing Your Luneometer

1. You will need a copy of the luneometer pattern on card stock, a 20 cm piece of string, a paper clip, a ruler, and transparent tape to construct your luneometer.
2. Poke a hole at the spot labeled *Plumb Bob Anchor*. Thread the string through this hole so that about 2 cm hangs on the backside of the luneometer. Tape this short end securely to the back.
3. Tie a paper clip to the other end of the string and make sure that it swings freely from the vertex.
4. To provide a sighting plane, tape the broad upper band of the luneometer to your ruler.

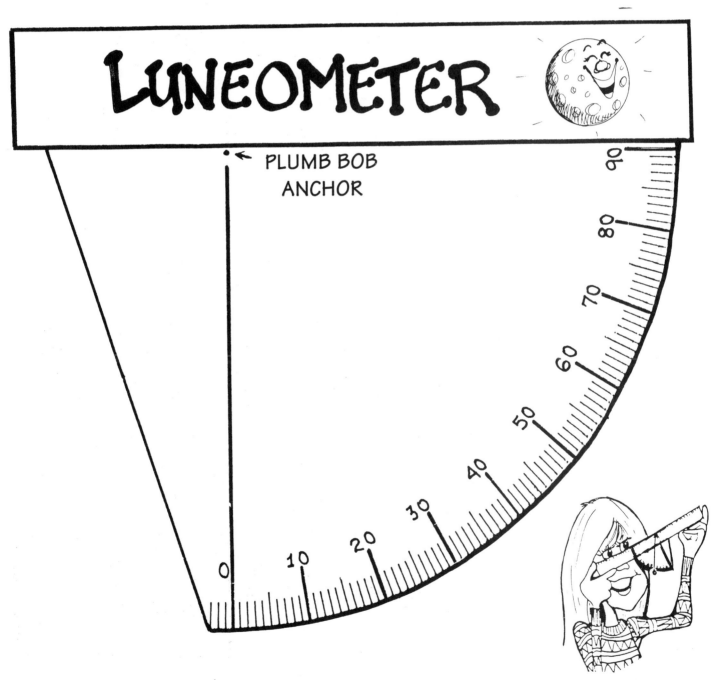

Stars in the Milky Way Galaxy

Topic Area
Estimating numbers of stars

Introductory Statement
Students will discover the method by which scientists estimate the number of stars in the Milky Way Galaxy by calculating the number of characters on a page in the classified section of the newspaper using a random sampling technique.

Math
Estimating
Measuring
Counting
Random sampling
Using statistics
    mean
    median
    range
Using proportional reasoning
Calculating

Math/Science Processes
Predicting
Observing
Communicating
Recording data
Analyzing
Generalizing

Materials
Per group:
    classified section of newspaper
    1 meter stick

Key Questions
1. How can scientists say there are about 100 billion stars in the Milky Way Galaxy?
2. Did they count them all?

Background Information
There are two principle ways of gathering data: by census or by sample. Since it is usually impractical to study every element, the preferred technique is sampling. For example, rather than count all the grains of sand on a beach, one can count the number of grains in a small area. Once that value is known, one can multiply to obtain an estimate of the number of grains on the beach. One of the most frequently used methods of sampling is *random sampling*. In random sampling, each element has an equal chance of appearing in the sample.

Management Suggestions
1. Student group size may range from two to six.
2. Six random samples is the minimum number required to get reliable data. You may choose to do more.
3. When counting the number of characters within the square, everything counts (letters, symbols, punctuation marks, etc.) If half or more of a character falls within the square, it counts.

Procedure
1. Since they cannot count stars during the day, tell the students that they are going to sample an artificial sky by counting the number of characters on a page from the classified section of the newspaper.
2. Ask the students to estimate the number of characters on their page of classified ads.
3. Have the students begin counting. After a short period of time, the students will realize that there must be an "easier" way. Ask them to suggest some possibilities.
4. Distribute the activity pages. Have the students record individual estimates of the number of characters on a page from the classified section of the newspaper and then average their group's estimates.
5. Have students measure the length and width of the printed portion of their page and calculate its area.
6. Cut out six 2 centimeter x 2 centimeter squares (4 square centimeters).
7. Lay the newspaper flat on the floor. Drop the squares onto the newspaper, one at a time, from a

height of 50 centimeters. Trace around the squares with a pencil.

8. Count the number of characters in each square. To be counted, at least half of the character must be located within the square.

9. Find the average number of characters per four square centimeters and per square centimeter.

10. Continue through the activity pages to determine the number of issues, the number of years of publication, and the wall spaces filled with classified ads needed to represent the number of stars in the Milky Way Galaxy. The students will finish by applying their collected information to 200 billion visible stars and to 600 billion invisible stars in dark matter.

Discussion

1. How many "stars" were on your page?

2. Did each group come up with the same number? Why or why not?

3. What event in history represents the length of time needed for publishing 100,000,000,000 characters in the classified ads? Compare and contrast the years and events with other groups in the class.

4. What patterns do you see in the table? Were you able to multiply all numbers by 2 and 6 respectively? Explain.

5. What happened to the year when publication had to begin with 200 billion "stars" and 600 billion "stars?"

6. Would it have been possible to publish newspapers in those years? Explain your answer.

7. How could astronomers use the principle of random sampling to count the number of stars in our galaxy?

Information Sources

The study of our galaxy is very dynamic with new information. Students should be conscious of this influx of information and encouraged to do research in the area. Astronomy is an excellent example of the beauty of science: As we learn more, we are constantly modifying our existing knowledge. In preparing this activity, the following current information was used:

Cowen, R. (1993, June 12). Nearby galaxy sheds light on dark matter. *Science News,* pp. 374-375.

Wiley, John P., Jr. (1993, April). Phenomena, comment and notes. *Smithsonian,* pp. 24-27.

Our Awesome Milky Way Galaxy

Step out during the early evening on a clear, moonless, winter night and you will see a faint milky band of light stretching across the heavens directly overhead. Known as the Milky Way, this band contains the densest concentration of stars in our galaxy. The ancients imagined it was a trail of milk across the sky left by a goddess who was nursing her baby. All the other stars you see also belong to this gigantic star system we call the Milky Way Galaxy.

The Greeks derived the term galaxy from their word gala which means milk. The Greek scholar Democritus was the first to guess the true nature of the Milky Way in the fourth century B. C. He wrote, "It is a lustre of small stars very close together." It remained for Galileo to turn his new telescope to look at the Milky Way in 1610 to prove that Democritus had guessed right!

The earth is one of the nine planets revolving around the sun, our closest star. But our sun is only one of the more than 100 billion visible stars in the Milky Way Galaxy held together by the force of gravity!

In addition to the visible suns, our galaxy contains large amounts of dark matter which, since it cannot be seen, can only be detected by measuring its gravitational influence on visible objects. Recent research has produced calculations that the Milky Way contains five to ten times as much dark matter as visible stars; that the total mass in our galaxy is equivalent to that of at least 600 billion stars; and that dark matter forms a giant halo at least six times larger than the visible disk of the Milky Way Galaxy.

The Milky Way Galaxy is shaped like a huge disk with a spherical bulge at its center. Its diameter is estimated to be 100,000 light years and its thickness about 2,000 light years. Our sun is about 30,000 light years from the center. A light year is the distance light travels (at its speed of 186,000 miles per second) in one year. If viewed from the edge of the disk, astronomers have evidence that our galaxy looks like this.

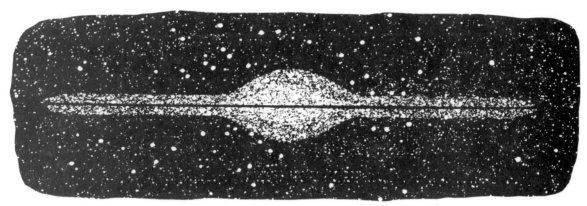

Our galaxy is revolving around its center. It takes 200 million years to complete one revolution. Since the earth is moving toward the edge of the revolving disk, we are speeding through space at a phenomenal speed!

Our galaxy has plenty of company. There are more than 100 billion galaxies in the universe! They typically consist of more than 100 billion visible suns with some having as many as 300 billion. Some stars are 100 times more massive than our sun.

Galaxies come in three basic shapes: spiral, elliptical, and irregular. The Milky Way Galaxy is an open spiral galaxy with its spiral arms wrapped around a nucleus. If we could view the Milky Way Galaxy from "above," it would look something like this drawing. Our solar system is located in one of the five optically-identifiable spiral arms.

Strangely enough, we know less about our galaxy than some of those farther out in space because we cannot view it from outside and are limited in our ability to penetrate it. Interstellar dust clouds prevent us from seeing very far into the Milky Way Galaxy even with the use of our most powerful telescopes. Today, most of the research is done using radio, infrared, and high-energy telescopes. Some scientists hold that a remarkable object, in all likelihood a massive black hole, lies at the center of the Milky Way Galaxy. Based on more recent evidence, some have theorized that the nucleus consists instead of a very dense concentration of stars, some of which are colliding. Intensive exploration of our galaxy continues and we can expect to continue to read about new discoveries.

Stars in the Milky Way Galaxy

Solving any problem in statistics involves three steps:
a. definition of the problem
b. collection of data, and
c. analysis of the data.

There are two principle ways of gathering data, by census or by sampling. Since it is usually impractical to study every element as required in a census, the alternative technique is sampling. For example, rather than counting all of the characters on a newspaper classified ad page, one can count the number of characters in a small area and then use proportional reasoning to mathematically calculate an estimate of the total number on the page.

One of the most frequently used methods of sampling involves random samples in which each element has an equal chance of being chosen. This investigation involves random sampling.

Your Task

Examine a page from the classified section of a newspaper. Your task is to determine the approximate number of characters on the page by using sampling. Each character (a letter, symbol, or punctuation mark) counts as one. Begin by making an estimate.

I estimate that there are _____ characters on the page.

The average estimate in our group is _____ characters.

Collection of Data

1. Determine the area of the printed portion of your page.

_____ cm x _____ cm = _____ sq. cm.
  length   width   area

2. Cut out six squares that measure
   2 cm x 2 cm and have an area of 4
   square centimeters.

3. Lay the classified ad page flat on the floor.
   While standing about half a meter from
   the edge of the page, toss each of the six
   squares onto the printed portion. All
   must land within the printed portion of
   the page to be considered. If squares fall
   outside the printed portion, toss them
   again. Carefully trace an outline
   around each square.

4. Count the number of characters in each square. Where characters are split by
   the boundary, they are counted only if half or more than half of the character
   lies within the square.

5. Find the average number of characters in a square.

Number of characters in an area of 4 square centimeters

Square	1	2	3	4	5	6	Total	Mean

Analysis of Data

1. The mean number of characters per 4 square centimeters is _____.

2. The mean number of characters per square centimeter is _____.

3. The median number of characters per 4 square centimeters is _____.
   (Need some help? The median value is the number in the middle of an ordered
   set. To find that value, arrange the numbers in increasing order and pick the
   middle one. Because there are six numbers, you will have to pick the middle two
   numbers, add them and divide by two.)

4. The median number of characters per square centimeter is _____.

5. How do the median and mean compare?

6. The range of characters per square centimeter is _____.

Why do you think there is such a variety of answers? _____

_____

Calculator Fun

Use your calculator to find these answers:

7. The calculated number of characters on the page is _____.

8. What factors might have affected the outcome?

_____

_____

_____

9. Using your data, how many such pages would be required to hold 100,000,000,000 characters, the estimated number of visible suns or stars in the Milky Way Galaxy, our home?

Number of pages: _____

10. If an average issue of the newspaper has 20 such pages, how many issues would be required to show 100 billion characters?

Number of issues: _____

11. If 365 issues are published annually, how many years of publication would be required to display 100 billion characters?

Number of years: _____

12. If such a newspaper had been published long enough to reach the 100 billion character level today, when would it have had to begin publishing?

Year: _____

13. Relate that year to an event in history.

_____

_____

_____

14. If the longest wall in your class room was papered with such pages, what would be the estimated number of characters on the wall?

Number of characters
on the wall: _____

15. How many such wall spaces would be required to display 100 billion characters?

Number of wall spaces: _____

100...200...600 billion ?

From *Our Awesome Milky Way Galaxy*, we find that many researchers believe that our galaxy contains five to ten times as much dark matter as visible stars. This mass, they believe, is equivalent to at least 600 billion stars. Other scientists believe there are closer to 200 billion visible stars in our galaxy. To try to understand these vast differences, fill in the chart to see what information we get when we compare and contrast the various viewpoints:

100,000,000,000 visible stars,
200,000,000,000 visible stars,
600,000,000,000 invisible stars in dark matter.

Number of stars	Characters per page	Number of pages required	Number of issues needed	Years of publication required	Beginning year of publication
100 billion					
200 billion					
600 billion					

List two things you find remarkable about your findings.

It All Depends On Your Point Of View
(It's A Matter Of Perspective)

Topic Area
Three dimensional properties of constellations

Introductory Statement
Students will discover that the star patterns seen in constellations are the result of the earthbound observer's perspective, or point of view, rather than evidence of any actual relationship between the individual stars themselves. This will occur as students construct 3-dimensional models of constellations, observe the models from different observation points, and compare results of their observations.

Math
Using number sense
Measuring
Graphing
Using geometry
Estimating

Science
Astronomy
   stars

Math/Science Processes
Predicting
Observing
Recording data
Comparing data
Generalizing
Analyzing

Materials
For groups of four:
   cardboard boxes (i.e.. copy paper boxes)
   1 spool black upholstery thread or monofilament line
   aluminum foil cut into 3"x3" sheets (8-10 per box)
   transparent tape
   scissors or craft knife
   large-eyed needles (e.g. #14 raffia needles)
   compass for drawing circles

Key Question
How can we construct models of constellations that will help us see that constellations exist in three dimensions rather than lie in a flat plane?

Background Information
Astronomers today recognize 88 constellations in the night skies. Forty-eight of these are the constellations named and recognized by the ancient stargazers. Constellations are star groups that form apparent patterns, similar to dot-to-dot pictures, to an observer. The shape of the patterns, the stars included in the constellations, and the figures represented by the groupings are not the workings of an exact science. Rather, they are the result of an aesthetic occupation; and one's imagination must be used to see, as the early stargazers did, the heroes, kings, queens, birds, bears, bulls, and dragons on the black ceiling of the sky. Different civilizations saw different patterns in the star groups.

These early constellations include the twelve constellations of the zodiac which mark the path of the sun, moon, and planets across the heavens; Orion; Ursa Major and Ursa Minor (which include the Big Dipper and the Little Dipper); Draco, the Dragon; Cassiopeia, the Queen; and Cepheus, the King.

Many new constellations were added to the skies of the southern hemisphere, regions that were not visible in the latitudes where the ancient astronomers made their observations. Some of these constellations are of less interest, having been composed to provide a scientific genealogy for the few inconspicuous stars occupying stray spots in the sky not covered by the original constellations. For astronomical reference it is often useful to have a map of the sky in which no black spot occurs. Thus, although the areas are generally poor in stars and often of little interest, they are necessary additions to the astronomer's system of mapping the sky.

Often, the newer constellations, especially those visible in the southern hemisphere, do not follow the ancient patterns. Rather than being based upon historical or romantic stories, they are named for such scientific instruments as the telescope, the sextant, the clock, and the microscope.

Whatever the name, whatever the pattern, each constellation appears the way it does simply because of our perspective, our point of view from earth. The heavens appear to us as a great domed ceiling, much as we would view the inside of an inverted bowel were we to be beneath it. As such, each star group appears to lie in a single plane as if pained onto the ceiling of the sky.

In reality there is not ceiling, the star groups are three-dimensional and each group would appear completely different (many would no longer be grouped together at all), if viewed from another point in space.

Through the activities in this lesson, this will become apparent and understandable to students.

Perhaps the best known of the constellations in the northern sky is the Big Dipper. In the strictest sense, the Big Dipper is not a complete constellation in itself; rather it is an "asterism", a group of stars that forms a part of a larger constellation; in this case the constellation being Ursa Major, the Great Bear.

86

The Big Dipper section of Ursa Major consists of seven principle stars, all fairly bright, grouped in a manner resembling the outline of a dipper or pan.

This star group is so conspicuous, and therefore easy to find, that it is known to most people. It is also one of the few star patterns that really look like the thing after which it was named. It is a circumpolar constellation, that is, it is in the northern sky above the horizon all night at most northern latitudes, so that it can be seen any night that the skies are clear and stars are visible.

Distances in space are so great that to give distances in terms of miles would be cumbersome and difficult to comprehend. Instead, astronomers talk in terms of light-years. A light-year is a measure of the distance light travels in one year, at a rate of 186,282 miles per second. That amounts to about; 6 trillion (6,000,000,000,000) miles. For example, it is easier to say that our closet neighboring star in the Alpha Centauri system is 4.3 light-years away, than it is to write that it is 25,000,000,000,000 miles from earth.

Management

1. This activity may take two class periods. Time will vary depending on students' experience working with graphs and construction of the models.
2. Students can work in small groups, or in pairs if enough boxes are available.
3. Make copies of the graph page.
4. Students need to be aware that the measurements given for the constellations are approximate, as are the distances given, but that they will be able to recognize constellations if they are accurate in their graphing and measuring.
5. All coordinates are given for graphing in the first quadrant of a graph to simplify the graphing process.
6. Use of craft knives for cutting the holes in the cardboard boxes is easier than scissors, but safety must be ensured by giving specific instructions and a demonstration in how to properly use such tools. Also, close supervision of the cutting process is recommended.

Procedure

1. Begin with a short class discussion on the difference between objects that are three-dimensional as opposed to those lying in a two-dimensional plane. Classify objects in the classroom (e.g. chalkboards, desks, chairs, charts, windowpanes, etc.) into the two separate categories.
2. Briefly compare a map and a globe to see how difference types of models are designed to show the same object in understandable terms, but using very different approaches (one-dimensional maps, three-dimensional globes).
3. Pose the *Key Question*. If, in the process of dis-

cussing possible answers to that question, some worthwhile suggestions are put forth, encourage students to try to develop those models.

4. Just as maps and globes show the same earth in different, yet accurate models, constellations can be depicted by different means. Students will first plot coordinates on graph paper and then use that to construct a three-dimensional model.
5. Students use the coordinates given in the lesson plan to plot the stars on the graph paper. You may wish to label the starts.
6. Calculate the distances from the earth to the various stars on the *Distance to the Starts* activity sheet
7. Fill in the graph page showing the relative distances of the stars from the earth.
8. Construct the three-dimensional model of the constellation according to the directions.
9. By sighting through the viewing hole on the end of the box, students will see the constellation as it appears from earth. The pattern will be recognizable, but the bonus is that the students get to see it in three dimensions, something they can not do when they view the actual constellation at night.
10. Have the students view the constellation through the side viewing hole and from above the box, which would represent views from other parts of our galaxy, outside of our own solar system.
11. Students graph of the constellation from these other two viewpoints by determining the coordinates for each star on the graphs in the background of each view.
12. Compare the two resulting graphs with the original for similarities and differences.
13. One of the great things about this three-dimensional model is that not only can we show how far each star is from earth, but we can accurately determine distances between the stars themselves. Have students find answers to the questions on the student activity sheet *Star to Star*.
14. Encourage students to use their imaginations and name their "new" constellations based upon their new perspectives.

Discussion

1. Have students discuss why they think the stars seem to lose their three-dimensional appearance. [There is a lack of visual reference points to give the stars their true 3-D appearance; the distances are so great that we are unable to discern the differences in distances between the different stars in a constellation.]
2. Can we construct similar models for other constellations? What types of information would we need to have in order to do so? What might be limiting factors in constructing such models? [In order to construct other models we would need to know the distances to each of the stars in the constellation and the relative positions of each

of those stars. Limiting factors might include great variations in the distances between stars which preclude the use of a similar model, at least in a cardboard box.]

3. Using this scale model, where would our own sun be in relation to the view hole (earth) as compared to where the other stars are? [The closest star in our model is 59 light-years away. Our sun is about 8.5 minutes away – about 1/20,000 millimeters from the view hole.]

4. Do there appear to be any relationships between the different stars in the constellation? What reasons do you give for your answers?

Extensions

1. Construct three-dimensional models of other constellations.
2. Arrange for a nighttime field trip to constellation finding. *Point to the Stars* has excellent information on how to successfully locate constellations, as do many other books in public libraries.

Sources

1. Joseph Maron Joseph and Sarah Lee Lippincott, *Point to the Stars.*
2. Donald H. Menzel and Jam M. Pasachoff, *Peterson Field Guides Stars and Planets.*
3. Robert S. Richardson, *The Fascinating World of Astronomy.*

The following information can be given to students to provide graphing experience.

The Big Dipper Information Sheet

Stars	Distance from Earth	Graph Coordinates
Alkaid	110 light years	(3, 101/2)
Mizar	59 light years	(101/2, 15)
Alioth	62 light years	(161/2, 15)
Megrez	65 light years	(24, 15)
Phecda	75 light years	(281/2, 9)
Merak	62 light years	(371/2, 131/2)
Dubhe	75 light years	(36, 21)
Alcor	59 light years	(10, 151/2)

DIRECTIONS FOR CONSTRUCTION OF THREE-DIMENSIONAL CONSTELLATION MODEL

1. Tape three sheets of graph paper inside the cardboard box in the following manner:

    a. Tape the graph paper with the plotted constellation in one end of the box.

    b. Tape one of the two remaining (empty) sheets of graph paper in the bottom of the box.

    c. Tape the third sheet on one of the sides of the box.

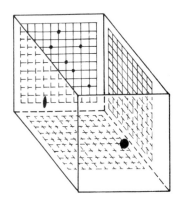

2. Cut a 1 centimeter diameter hole in the center of the box end opposite of the plotted graph paper. This hole represents the viewpoint from earth.

3. Using the sharp metal point of a compass (the kind used in drawing circles), poke a hole through the very center of each plotted star on the graph in the end of the box. Poke the point all the way through the cardboard.

4. Cut a piece of thread at least 25 centimeters longer than the length of the box and thread it through the eye of a needle.

5. Pull the needle and thread through the 1 centimeter hole towards the graph paper at the other end, leaving about 10 centimeters of thread on the outside of the box at the viewing end. Tape the 10 centimeter length of the thread to the outside of the box. (Running the tape lengthwise over the thread holds it more securely than just having one strip going across the thread.)

6. Cut and crumple a 3"x3" piece of aluminum foil into a ball (star) shape. Make the ball fairly compact, but not as tight as you can get it yet.

7. Push the needle and thread through the ball and then squeeze the foil more tightly.

8. Push the needle and thread through the star hole in the graph paper that is nearest the center of the graph paper (in the case of the Big Dipper, use either Alioth or Megrez). Remove the needle from the thread.

9. While applying slight inward pressure on both ends of the box, pull on the thread until it feels taut (tight) and tape it down in the same manner as you did on the other end. Release the pressure on the box and the thread should now be very taut.

10. Use a metric ruler to measure the distance from the viewing hole (earth) to the ball (star). By sliding the "star" along the thread, adjust the distance until it is the exact distance you calculated for the scale model. Squeeze the ball tightly to prevent it from moving.

11. Repeat steps 5–11 for each of the remaining stars, except it is no longer necessary to apply inward pressure to the box and the remaining threads go through their own stars, not the center star hole. Avoid having threads cross over one another as that makes viewing the constellation pattern more difficult.

12. After all of the "stars" have been put in place, cut a piece of paper about 3 centimeters in diameter. In the center of this paper punch a hole using a paper punch. Tape this piece of paper over the 1 centimeter viewing hole so that the actual viewing hole is now smaller in diameter. By so doing, you actually increase the sharpness of your view. Compare the view with both size holes and you'll see a difference in sharpness. (If you have a photographer in the class have him/her explain how depth of field is affected by the size of opening used. But, hey, that's another lesson in itself.)

13. Cut a 1 centimeter diameter hole in the center of the side of the box opposite the side with the graph paper taped on it. This will represent a view of the constellation from outside our solar system. Do not put in a smaller viewing hole in this side because you will be unable to see all of the stars from this angle of view if you do so.

14. You are now ready to use the model. Enjoy!

☆DISTANCE TO ☆ THE STARS☆

In order to create a model of a constellation that accurately shows the distance of each star from the earth, as well as from one another, the model must be made to scale. For this activity we will use a scale of 1 light-year = 3 millimeter.*By creating a model using this scale we can readily see the three-dimensional characteristics of the constellation and also determine the stars' distances from one another. To determine the stars' distances from earth in our model, we multiply the number of light-years times 3 millimeters. Each star is then placed that distance from the viewing hole. (e.g. If a star were 10 light-years from the earth our model star would be [10 x 3 millimeters = 30 millimeters] from the viewing hole. To determine the actual distance of the stars from the earth in terms of miles we would multiply the number of light years by 6 trillion miles. (e.g. 10 x 6 trillion = 60 trillion miles.)

STAR	Distance From Earth In Light Years	×	3 (1 light year = 3mm)	=	Scale Model Distance From Earth In Millimeters	Distance From Earth In Light Years	×	6 trillion 6,000,000,000,000	=	Distance From Earth In Miles
ALKAID	110	×	3	=		110	×	6 trillion	=	
MIZAR	59	×	3	=		59	×	6 trillion	=	
ALIOTH	62	×	3	=		62	×	6 trillion	=	
MEGREZ	65	×	3	=		65	×	6 trillion	=	
PHECDA	75	×	3	=		75	×	6 trillion	=	
MERAK	62	×	3	=		62	×	6 trillion	=	
DUBHE	75	×	3	=		75	×	6 trillion	=	

*A light-year is a measure of the distance that light travels in one year at a rate of 186,282 miles per second. That distance is approximately 6 trillion miles (6,000,000,000 miles).

DISTANCE TO THE STARS

# of Light Years	ALKAID	MIZAR	ALIOTH	MEGREZ	PHECDA	MERAK	DUBHE
120							
110							
100							
90							
80							
70							
60							
50							
40							
30							
20							
10							
0							

EARTH

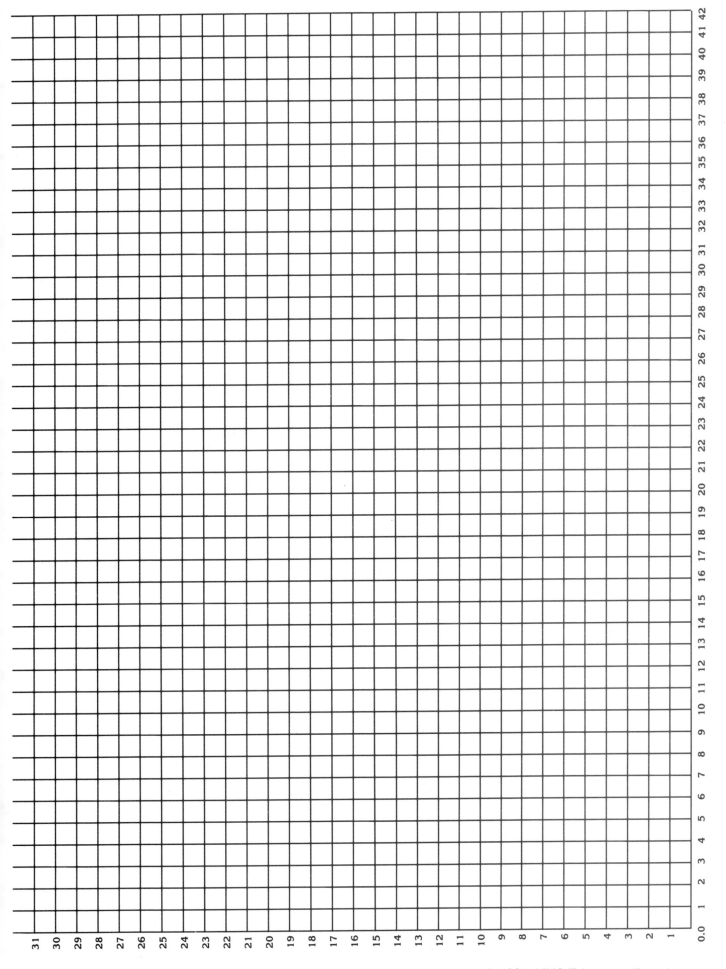

☆ ⭐ STAR TO STAR ⭐ ☆

We can closely determine the actual distances between the stars themselves. We can do so by measuring the distances between the stars and then converting that distance into light years. To do so, we measure the distance from the center of one star to the center of another and divide that measurement by 3. For example, if two stars are 100 mm apart in our model, we divide 100 mm by 3 to obtain 33⅓ light years. We can therefore see that the stars are actually 33⅓ light years apart.

Calculate the distance between the following pairs of stars:

STAR PAIRS	DISTANCE IN MM	÷3	# of Light Years Apart
MEGREZ - DUBHE			
ALKAID - MIZAR			
PHECDA - MERAK			
MEGREZ - ALIOTH			

By looking at the model and comparing measurements, find answers to:

1. Which two stars in the constellation are the closest neighbors?

2. Which distance is greater, the distance between DUBHE and ALIOTH or the distance between MIZAR and PHECDA? How much greater?

3. Would it take longer to travel from ALKAID to MIZAR or ALKAID to PHECDA?   If you were traveling at the speed of light, how much longer?

4. How many years would it take you to travel from MERAK over to ALIOTH, then to DUBHE and finally back to MERAK?

5. Both PHECDA and DUBHE are 75 light years from Earth. How far apart are they from one another?

6. Which two stars are 17 light years apart?

7. Which two stars are 58 light years apart?

ADDITIONAL RESOURCES

Young Astronaut Council
1211 Connecticut Avenue, N.W., Suite 80
Washington, DC 20036
(202) 682-1985

Astronomical Society of the Pacific
1290 24th Avenue
San Francisco, CA 94122

Hansen Planetarium
15 South State Street
Salt Lake City, UT 84111

Educational Programs Officer
NASA Ames Research Center
Moffett Field, CA 94035
(415) 965-5543/4

MIRA (Monterey Institue for Research in Astronomy)
P.O. Box 1551
Monterey, CA 93940
(408) 375-3220

BIBLIOGRAPHY

Asimov, Isaac. *Isaac Asimov's Library of the Universe: ASTRONOMY TODAY.* Gareth Stevens/Nightfall Inc. Milwaukee, WI. 1990.

Asimov, Isaac. *Isaac Asimov's Guide to the Earth and Space.* Random House. NY. 1991.

Beatty, J and A. Chaikin. *The New Solar System, 3rd Edition.* Cambridge University Press. NY. 1990.

Bonnet and Keen. *Space & Astronomy: 49 Science Fair Projects.* TAB Books. Blue Ridge Summit, PA. 1992.

Cole, Joanna. *The Magic School Bus Lost in the Solar System.* Scholastic Inc. NY. 1990.

Couper, H. and N. Henbest. *The Space Atlas.* Gulliver Books. NY 1992.

Curtis, Anthony. *Space Almanac, 2nd Edition.* Gulf Publishing Co. Houston. 1992.

DeBruin, J. and D. Murad. *Look to the Sky.* Good Apple Inc. Carthage, IL. 1988.

Eugene, Toni. *Discover Stars and Planets.* Publications International, Ltd. Lincolnwood, IL. 1991.

Gardner, Robert. *Projects in Space Science.* Julian Messner. NY. 1988.

Gibson, Bob. *The Astronomer's Source Book.* Woodbine House, Inc. Rockville, MD. 1992.

Hughes, David, ed. *Our Sun and the Inner Planets.* BLA Publishing. NY. 1989.

Hughes, David, ed. *The Distant Planets.* BLA Publishing. NY. 1989.

Jansen, M., P. LoveJoy, and D. Yee-Nishio. *Let's Learn About Outer Space.* Learn Abouts. Sacramento, CA. 1991.

Lauber, Patricia. *Journey to the Planets, 3rd Edition.* Crown Publishing, Inc. NY. 1991.

Littmann, Mark. *Planets Beyond: Discovering the Outer Solar System.* John Wiley & Sons, Inc. NY. 1990.

McDonough, Thomas. *Space: The Next Twenty-five Years.* John Wiley & Sons, Inc. NY. 1989.

Miller, R. and W. Hartmann. *The Grand Tour: A Traveler's Guide to the Solar System.* Workman Publishing. NY. 1993.

Moeschl, Richard. *Exploring the Sky.* Chicago Review Press. Chicago, IL. 1989.

Newton, J. and P. Teece. *The Guide to Amateur Astronomy.* Cambridge University Press. NY. 1988.

Pethoud, Robert. *Pi in the Sky.* Zephyr Press. Tucson, AZ. 1993.

Ridpath, Ian. *Atlas of Stars and Planets.* Facts on File, Inc. NY. 1993.

Schaaf, Fred. *Seeing the Sky.* John Wiley & Sons, Inc. NY. 1990.

Schaaf, Fred. *Seeing the Solar System.* John Wiley & Sons, Inc. NY. 1991.

Shatz, Dennis. *Astronomy Activity Book.* Simon & Schuster. NY. 1991.

Smith, P. Sean. *Project Earth Science: Astronomy.* NSTA. Washington, DC. 1992.

Wood, Robert. *Science for Kids: 39 Easy Astronomy Experiments*. TAB Books, Blue Ridge Summit, PA. 1991.

RELATED SOFTWARE

Adventures in Astronomy
Entrex

Elementary Math/Science, Vol. 4
Ecology, Astronomy, Arithmetic
MECC

Mickey's Space Adventure
Personal Computer Software
(Available free as part of the technology in the curriculum materials)

Planetarium On Computer: The Solar system
Focus Media

Space Adventure
Knowledge Adventure, Inc.

Space Mission Problem Solving
Orange Cherry Software

Your Universe
Focus Media

The AIMS Program

AIMS is the acronym for "Activities Integrating Mathematics and Science." Such integration enriches learning and makes it meaningful and holistic. AIMS began as a project of Fresno Pacific University to integrate the study of mathematics and science in grades K-9, but has since expanded to include language arts, social studies, and other disciplines.

AIMS is a continuing program of the non-profit AIMS Education Foundation. It had its inception in a National Science Foundation funded program whose purpose was to explore the effectiveness of integrating mathematics and science. The project directors in cooperation with 80 elementary classroom teachers devoted two years to a thorough field-testing of the results and implications of integration.

The approach met with such positive results that the decision was made to launch a program to create instructional materials incorporating this concept. Despite the fact that thoughtful educators have long recommended an integrative approach, very little appropriate material was available in 1981 when the project began. A series of writing projects have ensued and today the AIMS Education Foundation is committed to continue the creation of new integrated activities on a permanent basis.

The AIMS program is funded through the sale of this developing series of books and proceeds from the Foundation's endowment. All net income from program and products flows into a trust fund administered by the AIMS Education Foundation. Use of these funds is restricted to support of research, development, and publication of new materials. Writers donate all their rights to the Foundation to support its on-going program. No royalties are paid to the writers.

The rationale for integration lies in the fact that science, mathematics, language arts, social studies, etc., are integrally interwoven in the real world from which it follows that they should be similarly treated in the classroom where we are preparing students to live in that world. Teachers who use the AIMS program give enthusiastic endorsement to the effectiveness of this approach.

Science encompasses the art of questioning, investigating, hypothesizing, discovering, and communicating. Mathematics is the language that provides clarity, objectivity, and understanding. The language arts provide us powerful tools of communication. Many of the major contemporary societal issues stem from advancements in science and must be studied in the context of the social sciences. Therefore, it is timely that all of us take seriously a more holistic mode of educating our students. This goal motivates all who are associated with the AIMS Program. We invite you to join us in this effort.

Meaningful integration of knowledge is a major recommendation coming from the nation's professional science and mathematics associations. The American Association for the Advancement of Science in *Science for All Americans* strongly recommends the integration of mathematics, science, and technology. The National Council of Teachers of Mathematics places strong emphasis on applications of mathematics such as are found in science investigations. AIMS is fully aligned with these recommendations.

Extensive field testing of AIMS investigations confirms these beneficial results.

1. Mathematics becomes more meaningful, hence more useful, when it is applied to situations that interest students.
2. The extent to which science is studied and understood is increased, with a significant economy of time, when mathematics and science are integrated.
3. There is improved quality of learning and retention, supporting the thesis that learning which is meaningful and relevant is more effective.
4. Motivation and involvement are increased dramatically as students investigate real-world situations and participate actively in the process.

We invite you to become part of this classroom teacher movement by using an integrated approach to learning and sharing any suggestions you may have. The AIMS Program welcomes you!

AIMS Education Foundation Programs

A Day with AIMS

Intensive one-day workshops are offered to introduce educators to the philosophy and rationale of AIMS. Participants will discuss the methodology of AIMS and the strategies by which AIMS principles may be incorporated into curriculum. Each participant will take part in a variety of hands-on AIMS investigations to gain an understanding of such aspects as the scientific/mathematical content, classroom management, and connections with other curricular areas. *A Day with AIMS* workshops may be offered anywhere in the United States. Necessary supplies and take-home materials are usually included in the enrollment fee.

A Week with AIMS

Throughout the nation, AIMS offers many one-week workshops each year, usually in the summer. Each workshop lasts five days and includes at least 30 hours of AIMS hands-on instruction. Participants are grouped according to the grade level(s) in which they are interested. Instructors are members of the AIMS Instructional Leadership Network. Supplies for the activities and a generous supply of take-home materials are included in the enrollment fee. Sites are selected on the basis of applications submitted by educational organizations. If chosen to host a workshop, the host agency agrees to provide specified facilities and cooperate in the promotion of the workshop. The AIMS Education Foundation supplies workshop materials as well as the travel, housing, and meals for instructors.

AIMS One-Week Perspectives Workshops

Each summer, Fresno Pacific University offers AIMS one-week workshops on its campus in Fresno, California. AIMS Program Directors and highly qualified members of the AIMS National Leadership Network serve as instructors.

The Science Festival and the Festival of Mathematics

Each summer, Fresno Pacific University offers a Science Festival and a Festival of Mathematics. These festivals have gained national recognition as inspiring and challenging experiences, giving unique opportunities to experience hands-on mathematics and science in topical and grade-level groups. Guest faculty includes some of the nation's most highly regarded mathematics and science educators. Supplies and take-home materials are included in the enrollment fee.

The AIMS Instructional Leadership Program

This is an AIMS staff-development program seeking to prepare facilitators for leadership roles in science/math education in their home districts or regions. Upon successful completion of the program, trained facilitators may become members of the AIMS Instructional Leadership Network, qualified to conduct AIMS workshops, teach AIMS in-service courses for college credit, and serve as AIMS consultants. Intensive training is provided in mathematics, science, process and thinking skills, workshop management, and other relevant topics.

College Credit and Grants

Those who participate in workshops may often qualify for college credit. If the workshop takes place on the campus of Fresno Pacific University, that institution may grant appropriate credit. If the workshop takes place off-campus, arrangements can sometimes be made for credit to be granted by another college or university. In addition, the applicant's home school district is often willing to grant in-service or professional development credit. Many educators who participate in AIMS workshops are recipients of various types of educational grants, either local or national. Nationally known foundations and funding agencies have long recognized the value of AIMS mathematics and science workshops to educators. The AIMS Education Foundation encourages educators interested in attending or hosting workshops to explore the possibilities suggested above. Although the Foundation strongly supports such interest, it reminds applicants that they have the primary responsibility for fulfilling *current* requirements.

For current information regarding the programs described above, please complete the following:

We invite you to subscribe to $\mathcal{AIMS}$!

Each issue of $\mathcal{AIMS}$ contains a variety of material useful to educators at all grade levels. Feature articles of lasting value deal with topics such as mathematical or science concepts, curriculum, assessment, the teaching of process skills, and historical background. Several of the latest AIMS math/science investigations are always included, along with their reproducible activity sheets. As needs direct and space allows, various issues contain news of current developments, such as workshop schedules, activities of the AIMS Instructional Leadership Network, and announcements of upcoming publications.

$\mathcal{AIMS}$ is published monthly, August through May. Subscriptions are on an annual basis only. A subscription entered at any time will begin with the next issue, but will also include the previous issues of that volume. Readers have preferred this arrangement because articles and activities within an annual volume are often interrelated.

Please note that an $\mathcal{AIMS}$ subscription automatically includes duplication rights for one school site for all issues included in the subscription. Many schools build cost-effective library resources with their subscriptions.

YES! I am interested in subscribing to $\mathcal{AIMS}$.

Name _____   Home Phone _____

Address _____   City, State, Zip _____

Please send the following volumes (subject to availability):

_____ Volume V   (1990-91) $30.00   _____ Volume X   (1995-96) $30.00

_____ Volume VI   (1991-92) $30.00   _____ Volume XI   (1996-97) $30.00

_____ Volume VII   (1992-93) $30.00   _____ Volume XII   (1997-98) $30.00

_____ Volume IX   (1994-95) $30.00   _____ Volume XIII   (1998-99) $30.00

_____ **Limited offer: Volumes XIII & XIV (1998-2000) $55.00**

(Note: Prices may change without notice)

Check your method of payment:

❏ Check enclosed in the amount of $ _____

❏ Purchase order attached (Please include the P.O.#, the authorizing signature, and position of the authorizing person.)

❏ Credit Card   ❏ Visa   ❏ MasterCard   Amount $ _____

Card # _____   Expiration Date _____

Signature _____   Today's Date _____

Make checks payable to **AIMS Education Foundation.**
Mail to $\mathcal{AIMS}$ magazine, P.O. Box 8120, Fresno, CA 93747-8120.
Phone (209) 255-4094 or (888) 733-2467   FAX (209) 255-6396
AIMS Homepage: http://www.AIMSedu.org/

AIMS Program Publications

GRADES K-4 SERIES

Bats Incredible
Brinca de Alegria Hacia la Primavera con las Matemáticas y Ciencias
Cáete de Gusto Hacia el Otoño con la Matemáticas y Ciencias
Cycles of Knowing and Growing
Fall Into Math and Science
Field Detectives
Glide Into Winter With Math and Science
Hardhatting in a Geo-World (Revised Edition, 1996)
Jaw Breakers and Heart Thumpers (Revised Edition, 1995)
Los Cincos Sentidos
Overhead and Underfoot (Revised Edition, 1994)
Patine al Invierno con Matemáticas y Ciencias
Popping With Power (Revised Edition, 1996)
Primariamente Física (Revised Edition, 1994)
Primarily Earth
Primariamente Plantas
Primarily Physics (Revised Edition, 1994)
Primarily Plants
Sense-able Science
Spring Into Math and Science
Under Construction

GRADES K-6 SERIES

Budding Botanist
Critters
El Botanista Principiante
Mostly Magnets
Ositos Nada Más
Primarily Bears
Principalmente Imanes
Water Precious Water

GRADES 5-9 SERIES

Actions with Fractions
Brick Layers
Conexiones Eléctricas
Down to Earth
Electrical Connections
Finding Your Bearings (Revised Edition, 1996)
Floaters and Sinkers (Revised Edition, 1995)
From Head to Toe
Fun With Foods
Gravity Rules!
Historical Connections in Mathematics, Volume I
Historical Connections in Mathematics, Volume II
Historical Connections in Mathematics, Volume III
Machine Shop
Magnificent Microworld Adventures
Math + Science, A Solution
Off the Wall Science: A Poster Series Revisited
Our Wonderful World
Out of This World (Revised Edition, 1994)
Pieces and Patterns, A Patchwork in Math and Science
Piezas y Diseños, un Mosaic de Matemáticas y Ciencias
Soap Films and Bubbles
Spatial Visualization
The Sky's the Limit (Revised Edition, 1994)
The Amazing Circle, Volume 1
Through the Eyes of the Explorers:
   Minds-on Math & Mapping
What's Next, Volume 1
What's Next, Volume 2
What's Next, Volume 3

For further information write to:
   AIMS Education Foundation • P.O. Box 8120 • Fresno, California 93747-8120